KINGFISHER P.I.

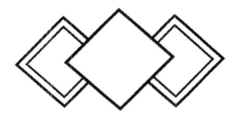

James Reasoner
and
Livia J. Washburn

Kingfisher P.I. by James Reasoner and Livia J. Washburn
Copyright © 2023 by James Reasoner
and Livia J. Washburn
The Book Place

All rights reserved.
ISBN: 9798863621685

Patient: Callista Kingfisher
Date: August 27, 3:00 PM

I really don't remember that much, Doctor. Falling, of course. I remember falling. I mean, it's hard to forget that feeling of going down and down and down with nothing under you, and knowing what's waiting at the bottom, and the seconds seem to take forever but at the same time they pass so fast . . .

Anyway, sorry about that. Didn't mean to get carried away. Thanks for letting me catch my breath. Obviously, I know what happened. I've seen the footage, and I've read the reports from the various safety inspectors and the agencies involved. I know we were on the fifth floor of the Crawford building, doing a fight scene on the girders, and I was doubling one of the villains. The girl I was doing the gag with was supposed to knock me off the beam and I fall five stories through the empty floors, since the building's still under construction, and wind up impaled on some rebar. Simple enough. The original plan was to shoot it on the second floor and let editing make it look like we were higher. But the director decided it would look more realistic if we actually shot the scene on the fifth floor. Kind of a jerk move, but no big deal. I mean, there's a net ten feet down to catch me. I've done falls like that from higher up plenty of times.

Yeah, that's right. The net never came loose before and dumped me into empty air all those other times.

I guess I remember more than I thought I did, don't I?

I remember twisting around and seeing that pile of insulation. I hate that pink stuff. Hate it. But being able to hit it saved my life. If it had been piled up a little higher, it might have saved me the broken leg and collarbone and the dislocated shoulder.

Yeah, mostly. Leg's still a little stiff, but I get around okay and don't have to use a cane . . . much. The places where the bones were broken ache a little now and then. I've had seven other broken bones in my career, though. That stuff doesn't bother me.

The memories of that day? No, they don't bother me, either, not really. Risk is part of the business. And I tell you, Doctor, when it comes to bad memories, a fall like that is nothing. I've got some—

No, no, that's not what we're here to talk about. It's still going to be a while before I'm recovered enough physically so the production companies can get me bonded and insured and I can work again. My lawyer said they would all want to have a, uh, medical opinion saying that I'm mentally fit enough to work again, too, so I might as well go ahead and get that out of the way.

Yeah, I almost did say that I'd need a shrink to sign off on me. Sorry.

No, I'm not going into that other stuff. I never meant to bring it up, and it's got nothing to do with what happened on that shoot at the Crawford Building.

Yes, I'm sure.

What do you mean, you can't sign off on me? I'm sane! I'm as sane as any girl can be who jumps off cliffs and buildings for a living.

I mean, how can you live and practice in L.A. and not *think that's perfectly normal?*

What am I supposed to do if I can't work? Yeah, I've got family, of course I do. A brother. Back in Texas.

Go home?

I suppose I could do that. It's been a while. The settlement from the production company was enough that I don't have to worry about working for a while. It's just . . . what else am I going to do? I mean . . . I work. That's what I've been doing for years. I don't know how to do anything else.

You're right, you're right. A few weeks won't matter. But I know what you're up to, Doctor. You think that by going home, I'll be forced to deal with those bad memories I mentioned a few minutes ago. Well, you're wrong, because none of that happened in Texas. It was all right here in Hollywood . . .

Yeah, I'll come see you when I get back from Corpus Christi. I'll call and make an appointment, first thing. I sure will. Count on it.

Chapter 1

Corpus Christi, Texas

The big guy on the motorcycle wasn't hard to follow. Joseph Kingfisher hung back a couple of hundred yards and kept him in sight easily. The man wheeled the Harley into a turn from Airline onto McArdle, then followed it to Rickey Drive and turned again.

Joseph was behind him, all the way.

The biker parked in the driveway of a frame house painted pale yellow with green trim. It had been a nice place once, Joseph could tell, but it hadn't been kept up very well. There was a small porch with a wooden railing around it, and the wood was starting to rot in places. The flower bed in front of the porch needed weeding. Paint peeled from the lowered garage door.

No cars were in the driveway. Just the Harley. Looked like Farrell was the only one here. This might be the best time to approach him. At his shop, there were always other guys around, working on bikes or simply hanging out, drinking beer and smoking weed.

Joseph parked at the curb on the other side of the street and got out of his car. Farrell had gotten off the bike and was shuffling toward the house. He started up the steps to the porch. Joseph called, "Excuse me," as he walked across the street. No traffic either way. This was a quiet time of the day.

Farrell stopped at the top of the steps and turned to look at him. If dictionaries still had pictures in them . . . and if dictionaries hadn't been replaced by phone apps . . . Boyd Farrell's picture would have been next to the definition of the term "outlaw biker". He had the beard, the leather vest, the chains, the black t-shirt with a beer gut under it and the cut-off sleeves displaying muscular, tattooed arms as thick as the trunks of small trees. The smart-ass part of Joseph's brain wanted to ask the man if he enjoyed being a walking stereotype, but he knew that wouldn't be a wise thing to do.

"Yeah?" Farrell said.

He didn't appear to feel threatened. No reason he should. Joseph didn't look all that formidable today in jeans, a polo shirt, and an Ice Rays cap tugged down over his dark hair. If he was being honest with himself, he knew he didn't look very formidable any time.

He came to a stop at the foot of the porch steps and said, "I'm looking for a guy who's supposed to live somewhere around here. Randy Garcia?"

"Never heard of him." No *sorry*, just the curt answer. Farrell started to turn away.

"What about Steve Clarkson?"

"No. What are you doing, taking the census?"

"I'm sorry. I must've got some bad info." Joseph reached into the back pocket of the jeans and pulled out some folded papers. He looked at the one on the outside and said, "Jimmy Marquez?"

"No."

A confused frown creased Joseph's forehead. "Boyd Farrell?"

"That's me, but I don't know those other guys!"

Farrell was annoyed enough that the words came out before he could stop them. His eyes widened, though, as he realized right away what he'd done.

"You've been served, Mr. Farrell," Joseph said as he scaled the folded summons onto the porch at Farrell's feet.

Then he turned to run back across the heat-browned lawn toward the street as Farrell roared a curse behind him.

Joseph didn't mind taking a few risks—it came with the job, after all—but Belton, Belton & Mendez didn't pay him enough to brawl with a bruiser like Farrell.

Unfortunately, he'd been concentrating on the ruse he'd been using to get Farrell to confirm his identity and hadn't noticed the old van that pulled up in front of the house next door. Two men were getting out of it, and they must have been Farrell's friends because he bellowed at them, "Hey, stop that dude!"

The two men didn't ask any questions. They just dashed into the street to block Joseph from his car. One of them, a burly Hispanic, spread his arms wide to make himself even more of an obstacle and said, "Hold on there, man. Our buddy wants to talk to you."

Joseph slowed to a stop and glanced over his shoulder. Farrell didn't look like he was interested in talking. He touched only one step on his way down to the ground. When he landed, he stomped toward Joseph like a leather-wearing tank.

"You sneaky little weasel," he said. "You know what you just did?"

"I legally served process on you, Mr. Farrell," Joseph said as he tried to watch all three men at once. He had his hands up in a defensive stance.

"That lousy ex-wife of mine runs off with my business partner, and now they're suin' me, tryin' to get the whole thing for themselves. Well, it's not gonna happen, see? It's not gonna happen!"

"That's a matter for the court to decide. I just served notice of the suit—"

"And now you're gonna pay for it!"

Farrell lunged at Joseph, reaching out for him. Joseph darted aside and made another try for the car, but one of Farrell's friends jumped in front of him and made him twist the other way.

Joseph had a pistol in the car, a 9mm S&W Shield, but with him surrounded like this, it might as well have been a couple of miles away in his office on Ocean Drive. He seldom carried the gun on him, anyway, because he didn't like firearms. Something about them—the noise, the smell of burned powder, maybe both—made him a little sick and disoriented sometimes. He preferred relying on his wits.

But in some cases, wits just weren't enough to prevent a

beating. Even if he wouldn't have used the gun, he wouldn't mind having it to wave in a few faces right now.

The third man yelled, "I got him, Boyd," and dived at Joseph.

Joseph almost got out of the way. A few more inches and the guy's grasping hand would have missed him and he would have had a clear path to the car. But instead, the man's fingers closed around Joseph's ankle and jerked his leg out from under him. Joseph spilled to the pavement, scraping the balls of his hands and jolting the Ice Rays cap off his head.

From the corner of his eye, he saw Farrell drawing back a workboot-shod foot to kick him. Joseph rolled out of the way. But even though he avoided Farrell's kick, he rolled right into the path of one from the Hispanic guy. The toe of the man's boot thudded into his right side. Joseph gasped in pain as he rolled onto his belly. The asphalt was only a few inches in front of his face. He tried to push himself up but failed. All he wanted to do was curl up around the pain in his side.

"I'm gonna stomp the guts outta you, lawyer," Farrell said as he loomed over Joseph.

"Not . . . a lawyer," Joseph managed to get out. "I'm a . . . private invest—"

"Hey, toadface!" a new voice shouted.

The shock of hearing those familiar tones gave Joseph enough strength to jerk his head up and twist his neck so he could look around. He saw the figure moving up quickly behind Farrell, who turned just in time to catch something swinging fast and hard across his face. The smack of the blow and Farrell's grunt of shock and pain filled the hot air, along with drops of blood that splattered from Farrell's nose.

"Who the—" the Hispanic guy began. The exclamation was cut short as the newcomer twisted away from Farrell, whose knees were buckling, and rammed the ferrule of a black cane in the man's belly. That was what the newcomer had used to hit Farrell, Joseph realized, holding the cane lower down on its shaft and swinging it like a baseball bat before flipping it to use as a staff.

The third man rushed at the newcomer, but Joseph was starting to recover now and thrust out a foot to sweep the man's legs out from under him. He fell hard in the street, just as Joseph had, which Joseph thought was fitting. Joseph came up on hands and knees, and before the man could get up, Joseph landed on his back and dug a knee into the small of it. That pinned him down long enough for Joseph to grab him by the hair, lift his head, and smash his face into the pavement.

The Hispanic guy was down on his knees, gagging and trying not to throw up from being hit in the belly. Farrell lay face down, moaning and moving around a little, but he looked mostly out of it. A small puddle of blood had run from his smashed nose and collected on the pavement. The third man didn't want any more, either. He put his hands over the back of his head and said, "Lea' me alone, lea' me alone," in a nasal voice that told Joseph *he* might have a broken nose, too.

Joseph's sister Callista grinned, held the cane in her left hand, and moved closer to him as she extended her right hand. She limped slightly, he noticed, but it hadn't slowed her down when she went after Boyd Farrell.

"Let me help you up, little brother," she said.

"I'm not your little brother," Joseph said in a testy voice, which was kind of a strange attitude to take since she had just saved his bacon.

"Yeah, you are," Callie said. "By five minutes, remember?"

Joseph ignored the hand she was holding out to him and climbed to his feet himself, staggering a little before he caught his balance.

"Five minutes isn't enough to count."

"Well, officially, though—"

"Callie, what are you doing here?"

"Saving my brother from getting his butt whipped, that's what I'm doing, Joey."

"Thank you," he said. From the sound of his voice, the words cut like razors coming out. "But I meant . . . why aren't you in California?"

"Can't a girl come home for a visit?"

"Of course, but you could have told me you were coming. And how in the world did you find me *here?*"

He waved to indicate the street and the three men lying there.

"Oh, that," Callie said. "I followed you."

"Followed me?"

"Yeah. I was going to your office, but when I drove up I saw you drive away, so I decided to follow you and see what you were doing today." She couldn't help but grin. "And you never even saw me. The hotshot private eye had no idea he was being tailed."

Joseph looked annoyed enough to chew nails. She'd always been able to get under his skin. She knew that and tried not to take advantage of it, but sometimes it was hard not to.

The big, biker-looking guy she had clouted with her cane groaned louder and started trying to get up. She said, "Maybe we'd better go back to your office and continue this discussion there."

"Yeah, maybe," Joseph said as he looked around. "Is that your truck?"

He nodded toward the Ram sitting there with its driver's door open and the engine idling.

"Can't slip anything past you, can I?" she said. "I'll meet you back there."

Joseph just jerked his head in another nod.

As he and Callie headed for their vehicles, the biker lifted his head and shouted, "I'll call the cops! I'll have you both thrown in jail! You assaulted me and my friends for no reason—"

Joseph stopped long enough to look back and snap, "Bull. It was self-defense. I had my dashboard cam recording the whole thing. You want to call the police, go ahead, but you'll be the one going to jail for assaulting a person legally serving process—"

The biker moaned and dropped his head to the ground again.

Callie paused at the door of her pickup and said, "I hope they get out of the street before any more traffic comes along. This must be an awfully quiet neighborhood."

"I don't really care if they do or not," Joseph said.

Chapter 2

Kingfisher Security Consultants and Investigative Services had its office on the fourth floor of a pink stucco building on Ocean Drive, just south of where the road turned into Shoreline Boulevard. It was an older, Spanish-style building from the Fifties, and its interior had always reminded Callie a little of the legendary Bradbury Building in Los Angeles.

She believed that was one reason Joseph had his office here. What better place for a private investigator to hole up? Although he never would admit to anything as fanciful as that, Callie was sure. All business, Joey was.

He unlocked the door and led the way into the office, which was just one room with a desk, a computer, three chairs, a small table with a scanner/printer on it, and a mini-refrigerator under the table. The bathroom, Callie knew, was down the hall and shared with the other offices on the floor.

"Still no beautiful blond secretary?" Callie asked as she followed him inside.

"No secretary, period. Why in the world would I need

one?"

"You have a reasonably successful business, don't you? Shouldn't you have somebody helping you keep up with the details?"

"Not really," he said. "Anyone who's well-organized can keep up with a lot more than they think they can."

"Yeah, I guess," Callie said. "You always did seem to have plenty of room in that head for whatever you needed to remember. That's how you got the good grades in school. A trick brain."

"There was no trick to it. Just a lot of hard work."

"And look where it got you. Serving papers on bikers who want to beat you up."

Joseph took off the cap and dropped it on the desk. "It's honest work, and it helps pay the bills when I don't have any other cases lined up."

"You don't have any other cases?"

"Not at the moment. Well, some firms have me on retainer to consult with them on their security systems, and some legal practices, as well, like Belton, Belton & Mendez, who had me serve those papers on Mr. Farrell—"

"An animal like that, and you still call him mister."

"He's a human being and deserving of respect."

Callie snorted. "What he deserved was a good, hard wallop across the face, and he got it." She frowned at her brother. "Wait a minute. You're not mad because I hit the guy, are you? If I hadn't stepped in, those three might have really hurt you."

"I was handling it—"

"No, you weren't. You can't seriously believe that you

were any match for them."

Joseph didn't respond to that, except to say, "Would you like something to drink? I have bottled water—"

"No bottle of bourbon in the desk drawer?"

"You've seen too many movies. But that's only to be expected, isn't it?"

That made her a little mad, but she supposed she deserved it. She made jokes about him being a private eye, so it was only fair that he could make jokes about her working in movies.

"Yeah, I'll take a bottle of water," she said. "That scuffle worked up a little thirst."

He opened the refrigerator, took out a couple of bottles, and tossed one to her. With a nod toward the client chairs in front of the desk, he said, "Sit down."

Callie did so and cracked the water bottle open. Joseph took the swivel chair behind the desk. Callie swallowed some of the water and then said, "No filing cabinets?"

"Filing cabinets are obsolete. All my records are stored on the computer and in the cloud. I know you're not a complete technophobe, Callie, so you should know that."

"Yeah, yeah. I just think that sometimes the old-fashioned ways are the best."

"Rarely," he said as he arched an eyebrow.

They sat there in silence for a moment, each sipping on the water bottles without much enthusiasm, before Joseph went on, "You look like you're getting around pretty well. Are you just about recovered from the accident?"

Callie shrugged. "I'm getting there. I don't really need the cane that much anymore, but the doctor says I ought to use it for another few weeks."

"I'm surprised you'd go along with that. You were never one for following doctor's orders all that well."

"I want to get back to work. The sooner the doctors say I'm okay, the sooner I can do that."

"Doctors?" Joseph repeated, having picked up on her use of the plural.

Callie made a face. "The lawyer who handles legal stuff for my agent says that I'll have to have something pronouncing me psychologically good to go back to work before the production companies will hire me again."

"I can understand that," Joseph said, nodding. "They don't want to go to the time and trouble and expense of hiring you, setting up a stunt, and then having you freeze up at the last second."

"Have you ever known me to freeze up?" she snapped.

"No . . . but you never fell five stories, almost to your death before, either." Joseph leaned forward, set the water bottle on the desk, and went on, "Callie, it was just a fluke that you *didn't* die."

"There was no fluke about it! I *aimed* for that pile of insulation."

"But if it hadn't been there—"

"It was. And I really wasn't hurt all that bad, considering." She sniffed, made a face. "I could do that gag again right now if I needed to. Wouldn't bother me a bit."

"All right," Joseph said, although he didn't sound fully convinced. "Whatever you say. I just . . . I hate the fact that I almost lost you, too. After what happened to Vickie, I don't know if I could—"

"There's no point in talking about that."

She saw the pain in his eyes and heard it in his voice as he said, "No, I suppose not." She hated him at that moment for even bringing up the subject of their sister.

Their big sister. The oldest of the triplets by four minutes. First Vickie, then Joseph, then Callie five minutes later.

Callie wasn't going to let herself think about that. Making her voice artificially bright, she asked, "So, how's your love life?"

"I've seen seeing someone, actually. She's a homicide detective. Nothing serious, though."

Callie arched an eyebrow. "Homicide is always serious, isn't it?"

"That's not what I meant, and you know it. What about yours?"

"My love life?" She laughed. "I've been busy recuperating. No time for anything else."

"And I've been busy with work."

"You just said you don't have any clients right now."

"As of less than an hour ago, when I served Mr. Farrell. Speaking of which, I need to get the Return of Citation form filled out and sent to Gary Belton . . ."

"So you want me to make myself scarce," Callie finished for him.

"I didn't say that."

"But it's what you meant." Callie set her water bottle on the desk, too, and braced the cane against the floor. Standing up was one of the times when she actually did feel more comfortable and secure using the cane. Once she got her legs under her, she was fine, but now and then she felt a little unsteady when she first stood up.

"Wait a minute," Joseph said. "Where are you staying?"

"I don't have a room yet. I thought I'd check at some of the places along the beach."

"Yes, I'm sure you won't have any trouble finding an empty beachfront hotel room on such short notice."

"Hey, the kids are back in school, right? The season's over."

Joseph dug in his pocket, came up with some keys, and tossed them to her. Callie caught them without any problem. She might still be banged up a little from the fall, but her hand/eye coordination was exceptional, as always.

"There's plenty of room at home," he told her. "Your old room is still empty, in fact."

"You haven't turned it into an extra computer room or something?"

"Of course not. I wanted it to be ready in case you visited. Not that you do that more than once in the proverbial blue moon."

"Hey, I've been busy," Callie said with a shrug. But she held up the keys and added, "Thanks, Joey."

"You can thank me by not calling me Joey. And you don't have to thank me at all. You have a right to stay there. The house is half yours, you know."

"A third mine," Callie responded, sharper than she intended.

Joseph just shrugged.

"All right, I'll see you there later, I guess. Maybe I'll fix us some supper—"

"Don't go to any trouble."

"Oh, I don't mind—"

"I said, don't go to any trouble."

Callie frowned. "Hey, I'm a better cook than I used to be. When you live alone, and your business requires that you stay in pretty good shape, you learn how to eat better."

"Fine. The pantry is pretty well-stocked. Knock yourself out."

"Like you would have been knocked out earlier if I hadn't come along when I did."

For a second, Joseph looked like he was going to argue about that, but then he said, "Fine. You're right. I might have been seriously injured. So, thank you, Callie."

This time, he sounded like he meant it.

Callie grinned, stuck the keys in the front pocket of her jeans, and left the office. While she waited for the elevator—which, not surprisingly in a building this old, was kind of slow—she looked out a nearby window that gave her a view of the beach, the L-Head, and the two T-Heads a couple of hundred yards north. Even though she had told Joseph the season was over, the beach still had a lot of people on it, and plenty of boats were tied up at the T-Heads. This part of Corpus Christi was beautiful, no doubt about it, and reminded her of some of the places she liked in L.A.

But, just like L.A., a lot of parts of town weren't so nice. The crime rate was fairly high, and although the traffic was nothing like that in Southern California, it often seemed like every other driver on the road was drunk. Before she moved west, she had been nearly run off the Harbor Bridge more than once. Yeah, there was a lot of ugly behind the pretty.

The story of her life, Callie thought as the elevator dinged behind her.

Chapter 3

The house was two stories, in the Spanish style like the building where Joseph's office was located, with a red tile roof and a large palm tree set in the alcove between the two wings of the U-shaped dwelling. There were more palms around the house and large flowerbeds that looked like they were being carefully maintained.

When Callie was growing up here with her stockbroker father and her high-powered real estate agent mother and her nerdy brother and free-spirited sister, the trees and flowerbeds and large lawn had been taken care of by gardeners, of course. Now only Joseph lived here. She wondered if he looked after the place himself or paid somebody to do it. She had no real idea how well his business was doing, despite her earlier comment about it being successful, but she suspected that neither of them could afford to live on the island if they hadn't inherited the place.

Located on a quiet street on North Padre Island, not far from the end of the JFK Causeway, the house backed up to the

Laguna Madre. Their father's sailboat was still tied at the dock. Callie didn't know if Joseph ever took it out. He had been a decent enough sailor when he was a kid—they all were, their dad had seen to that—but he never seemed to have any real passion for it.

Neither did Callie. She loved to swim, and she enjoyed fishing from time to time, but sailing wasn't her thing.

Vickie had taken to it and proven to be good at handling the boat, although Callie suspected that what she really liked was sailing past a boat or a dock with a bunch of guys on it while wearing one of her scandalously skimpy bikinis. She'd started getting looks by the time she was thirteen, and she liked it.

Callie told herself not to be catty, but it was hard not to have thoughts like that when she was standing here in the den, looking at the large photo on the mantel that showed the three of them on the *Lucinda*—named after their mother, of course—when they were eighteen, the summer between high school and college. The Brain, the Jock, and the Looker.

Callie's lips tightened as she thought about those nicknames. Their dad hadn't meant anything by them, except maybe as compliments. But then, he'd always been pretty clueless.

Correct, however, in some ways.

Joseph was valedictorian of their graduating class, with nobody even close to him. His test scores were high enough to get a full ride just about anywhere he wanted to go, with almost guaranteed success in law school. He'd opted for Harvard. Problem was, he'd hated practicing law, even though he was good at it, and quit to do something else. His contacts in the legal field made it pretty easy for him to get a private investigator's license.

Callie had been all-state in softball as a catcher, led the golf team to district and regional titles, put the shot and threw the discus in track, came in second in wrestling at the state UIL tournament in Austin. She'd had plenty of athletic scholarship offers but had turned them all down to join the Navy, which devastated her mother and prompted some speculation about whether she was a lesbian. She wasn't; she just wanted to do something she considered more worthwhile than sports.

So what had she done after getting out? Immersed herself in the world of make-believe, i.e. Hollywood.

Then there was Vickie. "Looker" was such an old-fashioned word, but it fit her. Men and women both couldn't help but gaze at her when she was around. She had dark hair like her brother and sister but with considerably more sun-streaks. A body that was good, although not overly impressive in any of its parts, but that fit together into perfection. A smile that befriended almost everyone instantly, and a husky voice that made everything she said sound like an intimate confidence.

It was too bad, Callie thought now as she looked at the picture of the three of them on the boat—Joseph in swim trunks and a t-shirt because he never tanned, just burned; herself in a white one-piece; and Vickie in a dark green bikini—that Vickie hadn't had any morals to go along with that beauty.

"Callie, you're being mean and petty," she told herself aloud, and she was. But that didn't make the thought any less true.

Or the pain of loss any less, despite that.

Callie blew out a breath, turned away from the framed photograph, and went to see if Joseph had any beer in his refrigerator.

Earlier, she had carried in her things from the truck and put them in her old room on the second floor. It didn't look exactly like it had when she left for the Navy. The walls had been painted, the carpet had been changed, and the bed was different. So were the curtains on the windows, which were on two sides since it was a corner room. But the dresser and desk were the same, and overall it still *felt* the same.

So did the rest of the house. Plenty of changes, but the bones were still there. The furniture, even though it wasn't what she remembered, was still arranged similarly enough that she figured she could walk around in pitch darkness just fine. Muscle memory would take care of that.

She had a pot of spaghetti simmering on the stove and was tossing a salad when Joseph came in. "Get that report filed?" she asked him without looking around from what she was doing.

"It wasn't a report, actually, more of an official form, but yes, it's taken care of. Gary said he'd put through the voucher for my payment."

"I thought you said they have you on retainer."

"They do, but I also get a fee for each service. The retainer just pays for me being available on short notice."

"What if you *hadn't* been available? What if you'd been

busy on another case?"

"They would have gotten someone else," he said. "Legally, almost anyone who's not a party to a suit can serve process in Texas."

"You mean *I* could be a process server?"

"Actually, yes."

"You don't have to be a private eye?"

"Not at all, although private investigation and security firms handle most of that sort of work because they're used to finding people and they're familiar with the laws . . . usually." He smiled. "Thinking about going into another line of work?"

"Not exactly," Callie said as she stirred the spaghetti. "But I did a good job of tailing you this afternoon. Maybe I have a knack for it."

"I wasn't expecting to be followed," Joseph pointed out.

"Probably a lot of the people *you* follow aren't expecting it, either." She paused. "Although, I guess cheating husbands and embezzlers are used to looking over their shoulders, aren't they?"

"There's more to the job than that."

"Right. I forgot about bail jumpers."

"That's part of it," Joseph admitted. "In fact, after you left this afternoon, I got a call asking if I'd be available for a job like that."

Callie looked at him with renewed interest. "Bounty hunting?"

"If you want to call it that," Joseph said with a shrug. "People who do that sort of work generally refer to themselves as bail recovery agents."

Callie put spaghetti and salad on plates, poured wine for both of them, and said, "Tell me about it."

Since it was just the two of them, they ate at the big table in the kitchen instead of taking the food into the dining room. It had probably been a long time since the dining room was used, Callie thought. Her mother had been gone for ten years, her father for eight.

She had thought more than once that it was a blessing they had passed before Vickie disappeared.

"The fugitive's name is Larry Don Barlow," Joseph said.

"Larry Don," Callie repeated, drawling the name. "Sounds like a good old East Texas boy."

"As a matter of fact, he is. From deep in the Piney Woods."

"But he skipped bail from down here on the coast?"

Joseph nodded. "That's right. He was arrested for delivering a bunch of stolen cars to a chop shop in Robstown. I'm not sure why he was all the way down here doing that. Maybe all the chop shops in his part of the state had all the business they could handle. But he failed to appear for his hearing, and the bail bondsman wants me to find him." He shrugged. "I told him I'd have to think about it."

"You're not going to take the job?"

"I'd probably have to go over to East Texas, since that's the likeliest place he ran off to, and you just got here—"

"Oh, no," Callie said. "You're not going to use me as an excuse for turning down a case."

"It's not really a case—"

"A job, then."

He looked across the table at her and said, "Look, you

wouldn't have come back here if you weren't having some sort of trouble. I understand, that accident must have been terrible—"

Callie put her fork down hard on the plate and said, "Don't try to psychoanalyze me, Joey. Me paying a visit to Corpus isn't a cry for help or anything like that. I just had some time to kill, and I didn't feel like staying in L.A. It had been a while since I'd seen you, so that seemed like a good enough reason to drive down here."

"Well . . . I guess I'm glad you feel that way."

"But I can go *back* to California any time," Callie continued. "So if you want to go hunt down this Joe Bob guy—"

"Larry Don."

"Excuse me. Larry Don. If you want to go off in the woods and find him, then by all means, have at it." She shook her head. "I'm not going to interfere with your career."

"My career will be just fine whether I take this job or not."

"You don't know that."

For a moment, Joseph didn't say anything. Then he placed his hands flat on the table and said in the reasonable tone that Callie sometimes had found infuriating when they were kids, "Why don't we just finish the meal and not worry about it? I told the bondsman I'd think about it and let him know in the morning, and he was fine with that. I'll sleep on it and see how I feel then. Okay?"

"You won't let me keep you from taking the case?"

"I won't let you keep me from taking the case. I promise." She nodded. "All right, then."

"This is excellent spaghetti, by the way. The sauce is

delicious."

"I got the recipe from a friend who owns an Italian restaurant."

Joseph smiled. "A friend?"

"Yeah, and that's all he is, so don't make it any more than that."

"I just want to see you happy, Callie, whatever that takes."

Chapter 4

She had been asleep for an hour, tops, when she bolted up in bed and screamed. The cry lasted only a second before she choked it off.

Please, don't let Joey have heard that, she thought.

But she wasn't surprised when quick footsteps sounded outside the door, followed by a discreet knock.

"Callie? Are you all right?"

"Yeah, I'm fine," she told him. "Just a bad dream. Go back to bed."

The door opened a little, spilling pale light into the room. "I haven't *been* to bed yet," he said. "I was just catching up on a few things." He moved into the room just enough to block some of the light. "You want to talk about it?"

"Why would I want to do that?"

"They say that talking about your nightmares can help keep them from coming back."

"What do *they* know? Anyway, I'm not sure I would call it

a nightmare . . ."

Oh, but it was. The same nightmare she had had over and over again.

Vickie showed up at her apartment on a Sunday afternoon. She hadn't let Callie know she was coming, of course. That would have required foresight and planning, things that Vickie wasn't good at. No, she was just there, ringing the bell and wearing that smile that said Aren't you glad to see me? Everybody's always glad to see me.

And when Callie asked her what she was doing there, her answer was, "Can't I come and see my favorite sister?"

Callie was supposed to respond, "I'm your only sister," but she didn't. Instead she said, "Well, come on in, then."

A little later, when Callie had poured wine for both of them and they were sitting at opposite ends of the sofa, she asked, "Where's Ron?"

Vickie made a face. "Ron is over and done with. I left him in Atlanta."

That was where Vickie had lived for the past couple of years, working as a producer in the news department of a local TV station. She had expected to be promoted to on-air talent, Callie knew, but that hadn't happened so far.

"I'm sorry to hear you broke up."

"Don't be. I can do a lot better than Ron."

The thing of it was, that was true. Callie had met the guy only once, but she'd thought he was a little on the scuzzy side. She didn't know exactly what he did, something to do with finances, but she hadn't liked him.

"I have a lead on a job out here," Vickie went on. "It's only weekend weather, but it could lead to more."

"Like I've told you, I can get you some auditions. I mean . . . Victoria Kingfisher. Was there ever a better name for a soap opera actress?"

Vickie made a face and shook her head. "More like a soap opera character. Anyway, are there any soap operas left on the air? They've all been cancelled, haven't they?"

"All but a few," Callie admitted. "Less than a handful, in fact. But there's all sorts of productions going on. Every streaming service has a bunch of their own series now."

"I'll think about it. But I'd really hoped to do something more, you know, meaningful."

Like smiling into the camera and reading the weekend weather forecast off a teleprompter, Callie thought. She didn't say it, though. No point.

"We'll see how it goes with that other job," she said. "Plenty of time to line up some auditions for other things later."

"Of course," Vickie said.

"You're the one who dumped Ron, right?"

Vickie looked at her like any other possibility was inconceivable.

"How'd he take it?" Callie asked.

Vickie sipped wine and shrugged. "I didn't ask him. When he texted me back, he just said okay, if I was sure that's what I wanted."

So she had broken up with him via text. That was no surprise, either. Vickie didn't like confrontation. Callie wondered briefly if she'd put news of the breakup on Instagram and TikTok, as well. She wouldn't be surprised.

But all that aside, it was good to see Vickie again. It might even be nice if that job worked out and she stayed in L.A.

Two nights later, as they were coming out of the restaurant where they'd eaten supper, Callie spotted a familiar face in a car cruising past. For a second, she couldn't place it, then she realized who the man was.

Ron.

He was looking right at them. Callie wouldn't have said his face was full of hate, but his expression was very intent. Then he looked away and drove on, and Callie started questioning herself. Was that really Ron, or just somebody who looked sort of like him? As for the attention he'd paid to them . . . well, she was with Vickie, wasn't she? And everybody always looked at Vickie. She knew, too, that she was an attractive woman herself and got her share of looks, even these days when a lot of men were scared to let their gaze linger too long on anybody.

Despite all that, she wasn't able to convince herself the guy wasn't Ron from Atlanta. The only thing that made sense was that he had followed Vickie to L.A. And that was worrisome.

She didn't tell Vickie about what she had seen, though. Vickie would just think she was mistaken, and even if she didn't, she wouldn't be that concerned about Ron showing up.

Two nights later, Vickie disappeared.

Joseph sat down at the foot of the bed. He might not have been to sleep yet, but he was ready for bed in pajama bottoms and a t-shirt; Callie had on the men's 2XX t-shirt she usually wore for sleeping. She frowned at him and said, "I don't recall inviting you to a slumber party."

"Look, you don't have to talk to me, but I really think you ought to talk to *somebody*. There's clearly more going on with this trip home than you're letting on."

"There's not," she said. Exasperation was making her angry. "And for your information, I already have a shrink. Well . . . a therapist. And all he said was that I ought to take some more time off before I go back to work. He didn't suggest that I come home or anything like that. That was all my idea." She blew out a breath. "Sometimes a cigar is just a cigar, you know."

"I suppose. I just know how you always liked to hold things in—"

"You want to know what it is that's got me messed up?"

The words tumbled out of her before she could stop them. Later she wondered if it was something about him being a former lawyer and a private detective that prompted her to talk. Some unspoken something, maybe the way he held his head when he looked at her, that made her want to tell him what was bothering her.

"It's being here that's getting to me. Being in this house where we all grew up, seeing that picture downstairs . . ."

"The picture of the three of us? That last summer?"

"Yeah."

"I like that picture," he said. "I take some comfort in looking at it. The world held such promise then—"

"Promises that weren't kept."

"It was our choice not to keep them."

"Not Vickie's," Callie said. "It wasn't her choice."

Joseph hesitated before replying. Then, "We don't know that."

"Yes, we do! She didn't just get some crazy notion in her head and run off again! Somebody *took* her, Joey. Something happened to her. That boyfriend of hers—"

"Ron Elgin was thoroughly investigated by the police and cleared of any connection with Vickie's disappearance. He had, well, an unbreakable alibi."

"Yeah, I know." Callie sighed. "He was in police custody when she vanished. And he stayed locked up for another four days until his boss bailed him out."

"And he had a legitimate business reason for being in Los Angeles," Joseph added. "Look, I wanted to blame him as much as anybody, but there just wasn't any evidence to indicate he was involved in Vickie's disappearance. Not even a shred."

Callie remembered the detective in charge of the case, a heavyset Hispanic woman, telling her that the two most likely explanations were that Vickie had been grabbed by a human trafficking ring . . . or that she'd been the victim of a serial killer, a sociopathic murderer who picked his prey at random. As beautiful as Vickie had been, she could have attracted either fate.

Of course they had investigated Ron. A spurned lover was always going to be the most likely suspect. But once he was eliminated, there weren't any other answers. Vickie didn't have any other friends—or enemies—in L.A. With nothing to go on, cruel, capricious fate became Suspect Number One.

And short of a miracle, or some hiker tripping over human

remains somewhere up in the mountains, there was nothing the cops could do and the answer to Vickie's disappearance would remain a mystery.

Callie picked up one of the pillows and hugged it to her, hating the way she gave in to that moment of weakness. "I should have been there," she said.

"You were on your way home. It's not your fault the shoot ran late. And it's not your fault Vickie decided to go to the store."

When Callie closed her eyes, she could see the note in her mind's eye, the words written on the paper in Vickie's careless scrawl. She'd been out of wine, and Vickie had taken it upon herself to drive the four blocks to the nearest supermarket and pick some up.

That was the last time anyone had seen her. At least . . . anyone who would admit to it. She had never made it to the store. There was no sign of her or her rental car on the parking lot security cameras. This day and age, it was hard to find a place in an urban environment that *wasn't* covered by closed-circuit TV cameras, but such blind spots still existed, and whoever had taken Vickie must have known how to make use of them. She was never found, and neither was her car.

Five years had passed. Cases had been open for longer, Callie supposed, but none of them would ever get any colder than that of Victoria Kingfisher.

CHAPTER 5

"Why don't you come with me today?" Joseph asked at breakfast the next morning.

"What?" Callie frowned at him. "Come with you where?"

"To work. I'm going to go see that bondsman about Larry Don Barlow."

"Why do you need me to go with you to see a bail bondsman?"

"I don't *need* you to go. I thought you might want to. You know, to see what I do during the day."

"I saw what you did yesterday. In fact, I helped you." She laughed. "Hey, I ought to get a share of that fee you mentioned. You know, the one for serving papers on that biker."

"I suppose I could do that—"

She held up a hand to stop him. "No, no, keep your money. I was joking." Then she grew more serious as she went on, "You just don't want to leave me here by myself. After what happened last night, you think I'll just sit around moping and brooding because of all the bad memories that have been stirred up."

After the dream had awakened her the night before, they had talked for a little while about Vickie's disappearance, but the conversation had been strained, with both of them full of painful reminiscences and the knowledge that in all likelihood, that aching loss would never have any closure.

"Well, isn't that what's likely to happen?" Joseph said now. He gestured at their surroundings. "There's nowhere in this house you can look and not be reminded of her. We all grew up here. You can't just put those memories aside."

"Some people could."

"Maybe. But not many. You can't." He paused. "And I can't, either. Having you here . . . well, it's like having an injury that's mostly healed up, to the point that most of the time you don't even think about it, but then you bump it against something and it hurts again. You've broken a lot of bones. You should know that feeling."

"My leg's that way now," she admitted with a shrug.

"See, you need to get out of here. You can shadow me." He snapped his fingers. "Consider it research. You're in a lot of action movies, right? Surely following an actual private detective around would be a worthwhile experience."

"I double mostly victims or villains," Callie said. "I've never doubled for somebody playing a private eye."

"But it could happen sometime."

"It could," she agreed. "I was gonna go to the beach, but I suppose it won't hurt anything for me to spend the day with my little brother."

He looked like he wanted to argue with her about that little brother business but gave it up as a waste of time.

◆ ◊ ◆

An hour later, they were back across the causeway, headed up South Staples Street in Joseph's car. Joseph was wearing a suit and tie today. Callie wasn't going to get dressed up fancy to go to a bail bondsman's office, but she'd opted for black jeans and a nice shirt. She had her dark hair loose around her shoulders instead of pulled back in a ponytail the way she often wore it.

It was an area of garages, paint and body shops, mom-and-pop cafés and *taquerias*, thrift stores, auto supply stores, plumbing supply stores, and, a few blocks away, the Nueces County Jail.

Location, location, location, thought Callie. She wasn't surprised that she had seen several bail bond agencies so far. You had to go where the work was.

Joseph turned in at a parking lot shared by a donut shop to the right and to the left a cinderblock building painted beige, with a neon sign on the roof that read *CORCORAN BAIL BONDS—24 HRS*. The parking spaces on that side were empty at the moment.

"Doesn't look like they're doing much business," Callie commented.

"Not that many people get arrested at . . ." Joseph glanced at the clock on the dashboard. "10:17 in the morning. They'll be busier once it gets later in the afternoon and then on into the night. This time of day is for catching up on paperwork . . . and business meetings."

"Like hiring a private eye to find somebody who's skipped bail."

"Bucko has skip tracers who work full-time for him, but he has to call in outside help now and then."

"Bucko?" Callie repeated. "The guy's name is Bucko Corcoran?"

Joseph laughed. "His real name is Bennett. He likes the sound of Bucko better." He reached into the back seat and picked up the briefcase he had brought with him. "Come on, I'll introduce you."

They went inside and found a middle-aged woman with graying blond hair sitting at a desk and working on a computer. She smiled at Joseph and said, "Bucko told me you might be coming by." She looked at Callie and raised her eyebrows. "And who is this?"

"Don't get your matchmaking hopes up, Gloria. This is my sister, Callie."

"Oh. Yeah, now that you mention it, I can see the resemblance. Sort of. Hello, Callie. Nice name."

"Thank you," Callie said.

"It's actually Callista," Joseph put in, knowing that she had never cared for the name.

"Thanks, *Joey.*"

He just gave her a wry smile and headed for a door, asking over his shoulder, "All right just to go on in?"

"Sure," Gloria said. "Bucko told me to show you in just as soon as you got here. He's going to be surprised to see two of you."

Callie wondered briefly if that was going to be a good surprise or a bad one for Bucko Corcoran.

She heard the loud, angry voice as soon as Joseph opened

the door to the bail bondsman's private office. In Hollywood, she had dealt with a lot of transplants from New York, so she recognized the accent as soon as she heard it. The Bronx, she thought. But she wasn't an expert on such things.

They stepped into the inner office. The man behind the desk glanced up and his eyes narrowed slightly when he caught sight of Callie, but he kept talking on the cell phone that was almost swallowed up by his thick fingers. He was round enough that the white Western shirt he wore gapped a little between the pearl snaps it sported instead of buttons. He wore a brown suit and had a bolo tie around his neck. His close-cropped brown beard and thinning brown hair both had gray streaks in them. The deep-set, baggy eyes gave his face a hound dog look.

"The judge gave you until four o'clock, Henry, but he ain't happy about it. You don't show up by then, he's gonna come down on you hard, and *I* ain't gonna be happy about that. You hearin' me, pal? . . . Yeah, well, I hope so. And don't you forget it. . . . All right, all right, you know what you gotta do. Live up to your word, my friend, or you're gonna be sorry. That I can promise you. . . . Fine. An hour, no more. You got it? . . . See you then."

He thumbed the cell phone's screen to break the connection and set it on the desk, then heaved to his feet.

"Joseph, good to see you," he said as he extended his hand. "I didn't know you were gonna be bringing a beautiful woman with you."

Joseph shook hands with the bondsman and said, "This is my sister Callie. Callie, meet Bucko Corcoran."

Corcoran shook her hand as well and beamed. "I should have recognized you, Ms. Kingfisher. Joseph's told me all about you, and I've seen plenty of your movies."

"They weren't exactly *my* movies," Callie responded with a smile. "In fact, they generally go out of their way to make sure you *can't* tell it's me."

"Well, I suppose that's the way the stunt business works." Corcoran waved a pudgy hand at the chairs in front of the desk. "Please, have a seat. Are you just visiting from Hollywood?"

"That's right."

Corcoran sank into the thickly upholstered chair behind the desk. "And you came along with your brother today because . . .?"

"I just wanted Callie to get an idea of what I do," Joseph said.

"I've never heard that much about his business," she put in. "It's more exciting than I would have thought. Dangerous, too."

Corcoran cocked a bushy eyebrow quizzically.

Joseph looked a little annoyed as he said, "I was serving some papers yesterday afternoon, and as it worked out, Callie was able to give me a hand."

"The fella you were serving took exception to bein' served, did he?"

"You could say that."

Corcoran chortled and slapped a hand on the desk. "I would've liked to see that! I'll bet you kicked that fella's butt, didn't you, Ms. Kingfisher?"

Callie grinned. "You could say that. And make it Callie."

Corcoran gave her a broad wink. "Will do. And I'm Bucko." He looked at Joseph. "Saved your bacon, did she?"

"I wouldn't go quite that far." Joseph shrugged. "But I was glad she happened to be there." He set the briefcase on his knees and unfastened the catches. "I'm going to take that Barlow assignment. I've brought along a contract—"

Corcoran held up a hand to stop him. "Hold on. Am I hiring one Kingfisher . . . or two?"

Joseph leaned back in his chair, frowning in obvious surprise. "Why . . . you're just hiring me, of course—"

"As you just said, *why?* Aren't two Kingfisher's better than one?"

Callie said, "I'm not a private detective, Mr. Corcoran."

"Bucko, remember? And you don't have to be a PI to work as a bail recovery agent, especially if you're working for a licensed agency, like Joseph's here." Corcoran nodded toward Joseph to emphasize his point.

Joseph took a contract form from the briefcase and held it up. "That's not what I had in mind—" he began.

"Why not?" Corcoran persisted. "You said that Callie's already done some work with you."

"Not officially, she has't."

As if he hadn't heard that, Corcoran went on, "And I have to say, she might come in handy on this Barlow business, Joseph. You know, help you blend in."

"How do you figure that?" Joseph frowned and shook his head. "We're not going to pretend to be a married couple. You can forget that."

Corcoran made patting motions. "No, no, that's not what I

was thinking. Barlow's father is in a rest home in Hackberry . . . that's the county seat of the county where he lives . . . and you two could claim you're checking the place out for your father or grandfather, or something like that. It would be a place to start, anyway."

"Well, I don't know . . ."

"And then if you got a line on Larry Don, you could go and corral him while Miss Callie holds down the fort at the motel."

Callie didn't respond to that suggestion, but she thought that if such a circumstance did come about, she wouldn't be likely to be agreeable about being left behind where it was safe. But they could deal with that when the time came.

Instead she said, "I think Bucko has a point, Joseph. Plus, after you find Barlow and take him into custody, you might need somebody to watch your back while you're bringing him back here. If he's a fugitive, he might not cooperate in coming back."

"I can pretty much guarantee that he won't," Corcoran said.

Joseph glanced over at Callie. "Well . . . I suppose it wouldn't hurt either of us to get out of Corpus for a while."

She knew what he was thinking. Out of Corpus . . . *and away from all the bitter, frustrating memories of Vickie and her disappearance . . .*

"Let's do it, Joseph," she said. "We've never actually worked on anything together before, even in school. Let's do this." She smiled. "It'll be fun."

"I don't know about that." He sighed as he slid the contract form across the desk to Corcoran. "But I guess you've got yourself a deal, Bucko."

CHAPTER 6

On their way back to his office, Joseph tried several times to talk her out of the idea, but Callie wasn't having any of it.

"We promised Bucko I'd go along and help," she said. "We can't go back on our word."

"Contractually, he just hired *me*. How I go about fulfilling the terms of the contract is up to me. Besides, legally —"

"Legally, you can pay me a one dollar per year salary and consider me an employee. Or put it down as contract labor." Callie laughed. "Don't forget, I work in Hollywood. There are creative ways to get around *anything*."

Joseph frowned. "If we're successful, I'll pay you . . . twenty-five per cent of the fee."

"You mean we won't split it fifty-fifty?"

"I'm the senior partner here."

"So we're partners now." Callie laughed again. "Kingfisher and Kingfisher, private eyes! I like the sound of that!"

"Well, don't get used to it," he told her, "because you're not a licensed private investigator. It takes a lot more than just calling yourself one."

"Maybe I'll stay here and do that," she said. "Maybe I won't go back to California. Stunt work is hard on the body. Jackie Chan may keep doing stunts until he's in his eighties, but I don't think I'm going to hold up that long. Being a private eye is probably less dangerous . . . despite that trouble you ran into yesterday."

He didn't respond for a moment, then with a cock of his head he said, "I do spend a lot of time working in the office on the computer. These days, private investigators don't get out and pound the pavement like they used to. I think you'll find that for the most part, it's dull, boring work, Callie. Once you realize that, you won't like it."

"If it's so dull and boring, why do you do it?"

"Because it's also methodical, and that suits me. I like sorting through things and putting them in their proper order."

"You can handle that part of it. I won't try to interfere. But if you need somebody's butt kicked, I can handle that part of it. Don't forget, I fought in MMA matches for a while."

"And had a mixed record, as I recall."

"Hey! I won more than I lost, thank you very much. Maybe not by a lot, but still . . . I might have stayed with it if I hadn't gotten into stunt work."

"There's no doubt you can handle yourself in a fight." He glanced at the cane which she had resting in the floorboard in front of the passenger seat and angling up over her left shoulder. "Even recuperating from an injury."

"I'm good as new," she insisted. "Next thing to it, anyway. You think old Larry Don will put up a fight when we try to grab him?"

"You never really know," Joseph said. "I've seen some fugitives I expected to be a lot of trouble come along just as meekly as you please. And some who look like they would never cause a problem will fight like wildcats. You have to be ready for anything. Which is another good reason I want you to stay out of the line of fire."

"We'll see," Callie said. "We'll see."

Bucko Corcoran had given them a photograph of Larry Don Barlow, as well as the contact information Barlow had provided to the authorities when he was arrested. Barlow's address was in a place called Hackberry. Callie had never heard of the town, so she looked it up on her phone.

It was in the Piney Woods of East Texas, not all that far from the Louisiana border. According to the phone, it would take a little more than five hours to drive there from Corpus Christi. Joseph stopped by the office on Ocean Drive to pick up a few things, then headed for the house on North Padre Island so they could pack for a trip that might last a week or more, depending on how long it took them to locate Barlow.

Callie had plenty of clothes for a trip like that. The night before, she had washed the ones she had already worn on the drive from California. She was putting them into her bags when Joseph came into the room and asked, "Do you know how to use a gun?"

She looked at him in surprise. "What do you mean?"

"Exactly what I said. How proficient are you with a gun?"

She shrugged. "I've handled plenty of them during basic training and on movie sets. They give us all kinds of safety lectures. I've fired more blanks than real ammo, though." She paused. "I've been to the range with friends quite a few times. So if you're worried about me squealing like a little girl and swooning just because a gun goes off, don't be."

"Do you have one with you?"

"Well, no." She shrugged. "I don't actually own one. That's not an easy thing to do in California, you know."

"I'm going to give you my Shield," he said. "It's small enough to carry without too much trouble. Texas is a constitutional carry state, so you don't need a permit."

Callie laughed. "Yeah, I hear a lot of talk in Hollywood about what a terrible place Texas is because of its gun laws, among other things. People believe you must have shootouts all the time, just like in the Old West."

Joseph made a contemptuous noise, then said, "You'll be able to handle the Shield just fine, I think. It's the one I normally carry, but I have several other options."

"Joseph . . ." Callie frowned. "*Are* we going to have to shoot it out with anybody?"

"It's very unlikely. But you never know, do you? Are you still sure you want to come along?"

"Oh, I see what you're trying to do now." She shook her head. "You're not going to scare me off that easy, little brother."

"Suit yourself. I'll give you the gun before we leave."

He did, along with a soft leather pouch that held the pistol, a belly band holster in which it fit, three magazines, and a box of ammunition. He was going to show her how to load it, but she did that skillfully herself, then positioned the holster at her waist and let her shirt cover it.

"I told you, I've used guns plenty of times on movie sets," she said in response to his surprised look.

"This is no movie."

For himself, he slid a Browning Hi-Power into an inside waistband holster and settled his shirt down over his pants. He put three more pistols—a 1911 and two short-barreled revolvers—in his bags. Callie watched him and said, "You act like we're going to war."

He looked at her and said, "I'm preparing for possible trouble. That's all. But this *is* serious work, and it *can* be dangerous. That's why I didn't want you to go. Don't want you to go."

"I can take care of myself," she said, a little annoyed by his protective attitude. "In case you didn't know it, I risk my life all the time."

"Yes, I've seen your limp and that cane you carry. That's why I finally decided to stop arguing with you. I know you can keep a cool head when things are going wrong around you."

"Well . . . thank you. It's nice to get a compliment from you."

"Don't get used to it," he told her. He snapped his bag shut. "Ready?"

"Let's go find Larry Don," Callie said.

◆ ◊ ◆

At Callie's suggestion, they took her pickup. Joseph agreed that it might stand out a little less in a small town like Hackberry.

"Just try not to get too many speeding tickets along the way," he said. "I know what a heavy foot you used to have on the gas."

"I don't have a heavy foot," she told him with a grin. "I have a need for speed."

With that, they climbed the new, towering Harbor Bridge and swooped down toward Indian Point to leave Corpus Christi behind them.

They stopped for lunch at a seafood restaurant in Fulton, up the coast from Corpus, and then continued on toward Houston, where they would circle around the worst of the traffic—hopefully—and then cut north into deep East Texas.

Callie was used to the traffic in Los Angeles, so Houston didn't seem all that bad to her. Apparently it made Joseph a little nervous, though, judging by the way his right foot sometimes pushed against the floorboard as if he were hitting the brakes. She took it easy as she followed the freeways around the sprawling metropolis. She didn't want to give her little brother a heart attack before they even reached their destination.

She hadn't told him that she'd done some stunt driving on a few pictures. That really would have freaked him out.

After a while, he dozed off, so she figured he must have decided to trust her. She didn't need his help navigating. The truck's GPS took care of that. She had a pretty good idea where they were going, anyway, having studied the route on her phone.

By the middle of the afternoon, her leg was starting to ache from sitting for so long. She stopped at an enormous convenience store with acres and acres of parking and gas pumps. Joseph roused from his nap and insisted on topping off the truck's tank using his agency's credit card. This trip was a business expense, after all, he told her. Once that was done, they went inside the sprawling store and walked around for a while, just to stretch their legs and ease stiff muscles.

Joseph offered to drive the rest of the way. With instinctive defensiveness, Callie was about to insist that she could handle it, but then shrugged and told him, "Sure, go ahead. I can see more of the scenery that way."

"There won't be much scenery unless you like trees," he said. "Pretty soon, that's all you'll be able to see."

He was right about that, Callie knew. She had been through East Texas before, through the Piney Woods or the Big Thicket or whatever you wanted to call it. Any area that hadn't been cleared for roads or businesses or housing developments was covered with dense growth. The pines towered high, shutting out some of the sky, and grew so closely together that they looked impenetrable. There *were* trails through them, of course, but she could imagine how easy it would be to get lost in there. If you were out of earshot of a road, you might wander around for days, probably in endless circles.

Joseph drove a little slower than she did, but not enough to be *too* annoying. They left the Interstate and angled deeper into the woods on a state highway that quickly went from four lanes down to two. The sun was still high in the sky when

Callie yawned and said, "This has been a long afternoon."

"And it's only a little more than half over," Joseph pointed out. He nodded toward a sign they were passing that announced it was 21 more miles to Hackberry. "But we're almost there."

"Should we go ahead and check out that nursing home where Barlow's grandfather lives?"

"No, it's late enough in the day that it might be best to let that wait for tomorrow. We'll find a place to stay, get a couple of rooms, and rest up from the drive before we start looking in earnest. We can go to the nursing home first thing in the morning."

"You know more about this stuff than I do, so that's fine with me."

They hadn't seen much traffic on the state highway. The pine-covered terrain was fairly flat, although there were some shallow hills with long, gentle slopes leading up and down them. Callie was yawning again as they crested one of those rises. She could see the road running straight ahead of them for about a mile, a slash through the thick forest on both sides.

Callie's yawn froze and Joseph let out a startled exclamation as something leaped out of the woods to their left and darted in front of the pickup.

CHAPTER 7

Callie threw her hand against the dashboard to brace herself as Joseph slammed on the brakes. The truck lurched hard, the rear end fishtailed from side to side, and the big tires shrieked as they left rubber on the road.

Callie expected to see a deer continue its mad dash across the road and disappear into the trees on the right side. She had seen more than one carcass alongside the state highway since they left the Interstate, leading her to think it was probably a good thing Joseph was behind the wheel since he was a more cautious driver than she was.

Instead, the rushing figure that came to an abrupt halt in the middle of the road was human. A young woman, in fact. She stared in shock at the pickup that had finally skidded to a stop about fifteen feet from her.

She wore blue jeans and a t-shirt and had blond hair that whipped around her shoulders as she suddenly jerked her head to the side to stare back at the woods she had come from. Her eyes were huge with obvious fright. She was running from something that scared her badly enough she hadn't even noticed she had reached the highway until it was almost too late.

It would have been too late if Joseph hadn't reacted as quickly as he had.

The road was empty in both directions. Joseph could have driven around the young woman and gone on toward Hackberry, but instead he turned the wheel and pulled off onto the shoulder. She hurried toward the truck and came up to the driver's window as Joseph lowered it.

"Can you . . . help me?" she asked, out of breath from exertion or fear or both.

"I nearly ran into you."

"I know. I . . . I'm sorry. I wasn't watching where I was going—"

Callie leaned forward and asked past Joseph, "For goodness' sake, honey, what's after you? A bear?"

Were there bears in these woods? Callie didn't know. But from the looks of the place, there ought to be.

"A . . . a bear?" The young woman shook her head. "No. But I . . . I need to get out of here. Can you give me a ride? Please, mister." She looked past him at Callie. "Ma'am? If you and your husband could just help me—"

"She's not my wife, she's my sister," Joseph interrupted her. He motioned with his head toward the door into the cab's rear seat. "Get in."

"Thank you."

The blonde opened the door and climbed in. Callie watched her closely. The fear she had displayed seemed genuine, but something this odd happening on a lonely stretch of road was automatically suspicious. The blonde could have stopped them so that her boyfriend could jump out and rob them, or something like that.

No, Callie decided. The young woman had come too close to being hit for that to be true. If she just wanted to stop them for some nefarious purpose, she could have stood on the side of the road and waved her arm to flag them down. Sure, some people wouldn't stop, but some would, even in this day and age.

Instead, she had jumped out in front of them and nearly gotten herself killed. That required sheer panic.

As soon as the blonde closed the door, Joseph pulled out onto the highway again and steadily picked up speed. Callie saw him checking the rearview and driver's side mirror and knew he was looking for any signs of pursuit. She did the same on her side but didn't see anything.

Anybody who'd been chasing the young woman through the forest on foot would have no chance of catching up. Joseph had the truck back up to speed by now.

"What's all this—" he began.

Then Callie said, "Uh-oh," as she saw two motorcycles appear at the top of the rise behind them. The bikes were headed in the same direction they were, coming fast. "Motorcycles can't go through this forest, can they?"

The blonde twisted around to look out the rear window and said, "Oh, no." She had caught her breath, at least somewhat, but she still looked and sounded scared as she glanced at Callie and went on, "There's a fire road back there, comes in about a quarter of a mile west on the other side of the hill."

"I think I saw it when we went by," Joseph said.

The blonde looked back at the bikes again. "They were on that. I cut across it, hoping they wouldn't see me, but they must have. They'll figure I might have stopped somebody and gotten a ride, so they'll be checking the traffic for me."

"And we're the only traffic there happened to be just then," Callie said.

The blonde nodded, her expression bleak. "They'll try to catch up, all right. And when they see me in here, they'll stop you. I'm so sorry. I never should have gotten somebody else mixed up in this. Just pull over and let me out. I'm the one they're looking for. If they have me, they'll let you go."

"Don't be ridiculous," Joseph said as he pressed down on the Ram's gas pedal. "We're not going to let that happen."

"You can't outrun them," the blonde warned. "Those bikes are fast. And they're probably calling ahead by now to get somebody to help them."

Joseph looked over at Callie and said, "Call 911. Tell them we're being chased by somebody who's trying to run us off the road."

"No!"

That exclamation made Joseph look at the blonde in the rearview mirror. Callie turned in the seat to frown at her.

"You don't want the cops to help us?"

"It wouldn't do any good." The young woman ran her fingers through her tangled hair. "You don't understand. You folks aren't from around here."

"No, but we want to help you," Callie said. "And we want

to understand. What's your name, honey?"

The blonde took a deep breath in an obvious but none too successful attempt to calm her fear.

"It's Julie," she said. "Julie Barlow."

Callie managed to keep the surprise she felt from showing on her face. At least she hoped she did. Joseph's expression never changed. He had more of a poker face than she did. His head didn't move except for his eyes flicking back and forth between the road ahead and the motorcycles pulling steadily closer behind them.

His foot pressed harder on the gas and the pickup surged ahead. Callie knew the Ram was capable of quite a bit of speed, but probably not enough to match those bikes.

One thing they had going for them was size. In any collision between the pickup and a motorcycle, the motorcycle was going to come out second best. The guys on the bikes *couldn't* run them off the road.

Would Joseph stop, though, in order to not cause a wreck that might prove fatal? Callie wasn't sure just how much ruthlessness her brother was capable of.

"I still think we should alert the police," Joseph said. "There could be a sheriff's cruiser or a state trooper not far away—"

"We don't call the cops much around here," Julie Barlow said. "Anyway, depending on who got the call, it might not help much. Those fellas back there have friends in the sheriff's department."

"They're not law enforcement themselves, are they?" Joseph asked, suddenly sounding a little more worried about what they might be getting into.

"Them?" Julie laughed, but the sound didn't hold any genuine humor. "Not that bunch."

The pickup went faster and faster, and when Callie checked the mirror on her side, she saw that the motorcycles weren't gaining as quickly as they had been. But they weren't falling back, either.

Luckily, the stretch of road they were on was straight as a string, so Joseph was able to coax as much speed as he could out of the Ram's powerful engine. But they were headed back up a gentle slope now, and Callie had no idea what was on the other side. If they encountered any twists and turns in the road, the bikes would be able to use their greater maneuverability to their advantage.

Joseph must have been thinking the same thing, because he asked, "What are we coming up on? What's on the other side of this little hill?"

"The road curves down to some bottom land along Samuels Creek," Julie said.

"It's not a straightaway anymore."

"Not for several miles."

Joseph sighed. "Are there any businesses? Places where people might be around? I assume those men chasing you might back off if there were more witnesses?"

"They might," Julie allowed. "Or they might not, depending on how bad their mood is. Wait a minute . . . Froggy's!"

"What?" Callie said.

"Froggy's. It's a café and dance hall and motel. About a mile and a half from here. If we can get there ahead of them, it's considered kind of neutral territory."

"Nothing closer?" Joseph asked.

"No, not a thing."

"We'll try for it, then." The corners of his mouth quirked in a faint smile. "That's about all we can do."

Julie's mention of neutrality made Callie wonder exactly what was going on here. That concept implied two hostile forces. She was already extremely curious whether the young blonde was related to Larry Don Barlow. It seemed almost impossible that she *wouldn't* be.

Callie glanced in the side mirror again and saw that the bikes were a little closer. The long uphill slant had slowed the pickup slightly. But they still had a lead on the motorcycles . . . for now.

She turned in the seat to look back at Julie again. "Why are those guys after you?"

"They, uh . . . one of them's always liked me, and the other one's his buddy." Her face turned pink. "They figured they'd grab me and carry me off to this shack in the woods where they hang out and . . . well . . ."

Despite the blush on Julie's face, which looked real enough, Callie had a hunch that the blonde wasn't telling the truth. Not all of the truth, anyway. Her instincts told her that the two guys on bikes had more in mind than some backwoods loving.

But as long as they were chasing the pickup, their motives didn't really matter. The only important thing was getting away from them.

The Ram topped the little rise going so fast that for a second Callie thought they were going to go airborne, like a chase scene in a movie. The truck's big tires continued to hug the ground, though. As they started down the slope, the road curved to the right. It wasn't much of a bend, but Joseph had to slow down a little anyway. The road straightened, but a hundred yards farther on, it curved back to the left, sharper this time so Joseph had to brake even more.

Callie looked in the mirror and saw the bikes sweeping around the turns, the riders and machines leaning far to the side so that it seemed like they might go out of control at any time.

But those boys knew what they were doing. The bikes came back up and blasted on. Taking the curve that fast had cut into the pickup's lead by a significant amount.

"How many more of these bends are there?" Joseph asked with his lips tight.

"Three or four," Julie answered, "and then the bridge over Samuels Creek and Froggy's is just on the other side."

Callie saw a yellow *Load Zoned Bridge Ahead* sign flash past. They were moving too fast for her to read the rest of the printing that explained how heavy a load the bridge was zoned for, but that didn't matter. The pickup wasn't too heavy to cross it . . . if they could get there.

Joseph piloted the Ram through another big S-curve between thick stands of pine. By the time they came out of it into another short straightaway, the motorcycles were only fifty yards behind them and still closing in.

"One more bend, then the bridge, then Froggy's," Julie said from the rear seat. She sat on the forward edge of it, one hand resting on the back of the bench seat as she twisted her head back and forth to look in front of and behind them. "We might be able to—"

She broke off with a gasp as she gazed through the windshield. A hundred yards away, where the last bend before the creek began, another vehicle had appeared, coming so fast around the curve that its rear end swayed a little as it straightened out and barreled toward them.

"More Wolvertons!" Julie cried.

Chapter 8

Callie didn't know who the Wolvertons were, but she would have been willing to bet they had some connection with those guys on the motorcycles. The vehicle rumbling toward them was a big work truck with a flat metal bed behind the cab. Not very speedy, but it didn't need to be in this situation. With no other traffic on the road, it could straddle the center line as it roared toward them.

"Are there any side roads?" Joseph called to Julie. "Anywhere to get out of its way?"

"No! They're going to ram us!"

That was certainly what it looked like. As long as the truck stayed in the middle of the road, there wasn't enough room to get past it on either of the narrow shoulders. Not far from the edge of the pavement, the ground dropped off sharply into ditches on both sides of the highway.

The gap between the two vehicles was vanishing with every second that darted past. And as big and heavy as the

Ram was, Callie knew that *it* would come off second best in a collision with that behemoth lumbering toward them.

Joseph slammed his foot against the brake and yanked the wheel to the left as he yelled, "Callie! Window down!" The rear end drifted right and ahead as the pickup skidded to a stop across the center line.

Callie hadn't stopped to think. She just jabbed her finger against the power window button and sent the glass beside her humming down. She saw Joseph reach under his shirt and knew what was going to happen next. She ducked without being told to.

He pulled the Browning from its holster, leveled it across the front seat, and opened fire through the window Callie had just lowered. The roar inside the Ram's cab was like giant fists pounding against Callie's ears, even though she had clapped her hands over them. The onrushing truck was so close it seemed like some huge, charging beast.

Its windshield wasn't bulletproof. The glass shattered under the onslaught of 9mm rounds. But with all those tons of metal hurtling at her, Callie felt like she might not survive more than another second or two.

Then the truck swerved to its left, and Joseph hit the gas. The Ram practically leaped forward the other way. Most of it wound up off the shoulder on the slanted embankment, close to the dropoff into the ditch. Callie thought she heard somebody screaming, but she didn't know if it was her or Julie or both. Or if the sound was even real. She was probably deaf from the gunshots, she thought wildly, and imagining the screams.

The truck thundered past them, missing the pickup's rear end by inches. Callie jerked upright and twisted around to watch through the Ram's rear window as the work truck slewed back and forth. Whoever was at the wheel was fighting to bring it back under control.

The motorcycles had continued racing after the pickup, but suddenly the truck was between them and their quarry. They peeled to the sides, trying to avoid the truck. One rider made it and stayed upright. The other lost control of his bike and had to lay it down. Sparks flew as the bike scraped along the pavement. Its rider rolled after it. Long hair whipped around his head. He hadn't been wearing a helmet. They hadn't been close enough for Callie to see that until now.

She wondered if he had hit his head on the road and wouldn't be getting back up again. She hoped that wasn't the case . . . but after they had chased her and her brother and Julie Barlow into the path of that murderous truck, she didn't care *that* much.

For a second, Callie thought the pursuer who had managed to stay on his bike might still come after them, but instead the man whipped around in a turn and headed back toward the fallen rider.

"Go!" she said to Joseph. "We'd better get out of here while we can!"

"That's what I was thinking," he said. He gunned the engine. The pickup's rear wheels were still on the pavement, so he was able to back up, turn the wheel, and take off in another squealing, rubber-burning getaway.

◆ ◊ ◆

A yellow *Narrow Bridge* sign sat on the side of the road about fifty yards from the bridge over Samuels Creek. The stream's name was on a green sign attached to the bridge itself. Samuels Creek didn't amount to much: a shallow gully with a little trickle of water in the bottom of it.

Not far beyond it, a large gravel parking area opened to the right of the highway. Behind the parking area was a rustic building with a sign announcing *LAZY PINES MOTEL* on its roof. Neon in the front windows spelled out *Office* and *Vacancy*.

Behind the office building, a dozen equally rustic cottages were laid out in a U-shape, four on each side, each with a carport beside it. In the center of the courtyard formed by the cottages was a small, grassy play area with a swing set, a slide, and a concrete picnic table flanked by concrete benches. No swimming pool.

Callie took all that in with a glance and figured the motel had been built in the 1950s, if not earlier. She made a quick count. Eight of the twelve carports had a vehicle parked under it, so there ought to still be four cabins vacant.

Not that she and Joseph would be staying here. Not this close to where they had almost been squashed like bugs on the front of that monster truck.

At the far end of the parking lot was a long, narrow wooden building painted dark green so that it almost blended in with the pines that formed a backdrop. The sign on its roof read *FROGGY'S CAFÉ—GOOD EATS.* Another building butted up against the center of it from behind. It was bigger, almost barn-like, and had an entrance on the side facing the motel. That would be the dance hall Julie had mentioned, Callie thought. It didn't have a sign on it, probably because, unlike the café and the motel, it catered more to the local trade, rather than travelers, and folks who lived around here already knew about it.

"Pull up in front of the café," Julie told Joseph.

"That's pretty obvious," he said. "If the fellows in that truck turn around and come looking for us, they won't have any trouble spotting this pickup."

"Oh, they'll come looking for us," Julie said, "but they won't do anything. Not at Froggy's."

As Joseph brought the Ram to a stop next to a couple of cars already parked there, Callie said, "I hope you're right about that. My ears haven't stopped ringing yet."

But at least her hearing had come back, she told herself. The shots from Joseph's Browning hadn't permanently deafened any of them.

Julie seemed a little shaky when she climbed out of the pickup. Joseph took hold of her arm to steady her. He looked surprisingly calm and composed, Callie thought. Nearly getting crushed by that truck didn't seem to have bothered him. And he had been not only quick-thinking but also very cool-headed to have come up with the strategy to save them in a matter of split-seconds.

Of course, some luck had been involved, too. Quite a bit of luck, in fact. If that truck had swerved the other direction, Callie wasn't sure her brother could have thrown the Ram into reverse and gunned the engine quickly enough to avoid a crash.

But it hadn't happened that way, so there wasn't any point in dwelling on might have beens. She and Joseph walked to the café's entrance with Julie between them.

The café was the same vintage as the motel, probably built at the same time. Probably for the same owner. For all she knew, Callie reminded herself, that could have been Froggy. She didn't know if the original Froggy was still alive, or how old he might be if he was.

Booths lined the front wall beside the windows on both sides of the double glass doors at the entrance. A counter with a formica top and chrome trim ran most of the length of the back wall, stopping just short of two doors, one with an *Employees Only* sign on it that probably led to the kitchen, the other with *Restrooms* painted on it in fancy gilt script. Stools with circular, revolving leather seats lined up like soldiers in front of the counter. Several booths were occupied by couples, and half a dozen men sat at the counter with empty stools between them to show that they weren't together.

On the far right end of the counter, the other end from the restrooms, sat an old-fashioned cash register. Next to it was a glass display case with pieces of several different kinds of pie on saucers inside it. If it weren't for the fact that at least three-fourths of the customers were staring fixedly at the phones in their hands, Callie would have almost felt like she had been transported back more than half a century in time.

A huge man with thin white hair stood behind the counter. He wore a white apron over blue jeans and a flannel shirt. He peered through thick-lensed glasses at the newcomers and said, "Julie, you look upset. What's wrong?"

One of the gimme-cap-wearing men at the counter glanced at them, then stood up and moved over a couple of stools so the three of them could sit together. Julie said, "Thanks, Hoyt," which the man acknowledged with a curt, silent nod.

They sat down. The big, white-haired man planted himself in front of them and rested hands with long, thick fingers on the formica. He didn't say anything else, but he looked intently at Julie as he waited for an answer to his question.

"I ran into Tom and Jimmy Wolverton," she said. "They thought I ought to go party with them at their place. I got away from them, and then these two folks"—she nodded right and left at Callie and Joseph—"gave me a hand." She smiled and went on, "I just realized I don't even know your names."

"I'm Joseph Kingfisher," he said. "This is my sister Callie."

Since he hadn't called her Callista, she didn't bring up the nickname Joey.

"I'm mighty pleased to meet you. More than you know."

The white-haired man said, "I'll bet Tom and Jimmy didn't take it kindly when you ran off."

"No, they didn't, Froggy. They came after me on those bikes of theirs."

A frown creased Froggy's forehead. "And I'll bet that had something to do with Earl and Norman running out of here a little while ago after Earl got a call on his phone."

"They tried to stop us in their truck."

"And you got past them?" Froggy sounded like he found that hard to believe. As she remembered what had happened, Callie thought the possibility was a little dubious, too . . . and she had lived through it.

"Barely."

Froggy thought about it and nodded slowly. "Where are those old boys now?"

"I don't know," Julie said with a shake of her head. Callie noticed she didn't add that some of the Wolvertons might be injured, or even dead, what with Joseph shooting out their truck's windshield and one of the bikers having to lay down his ride.

"Well, you're safe enough here. Why don't you call your uncle to come and get you?"

"I lost my phone while I was running away from Tom and Jimmy."

"Well, shoot, girl, any of these ol' boys in here will let you borrow his phone."

As if to prove Froggy's words, several of the men in the café stood up and came toward her, holding out a variety of cell phones.

Froggy made shooing motions at the men with one hand and used the other to pull a phone from a pocket somewhere under the apron.

"You can just use mine," he said, then lifted his head to look past the three of them at something outside the café.

Callie swiveled around quickly on the stool, expecting to see the motorcycles or the big work truck. Possibly all of them.

Instead she saw a white SUV with lights mounted on its roof pulling through the gravel parking lot, and behind her Froggy said, "Or maybe you can get Howard Whitfield to take you home."

Chapter 9

The SUV was a sheriff's department vehicle, Callie noted as it drove past the entrance to find a parking place on the far side of the lot. For a moment she felt better about the chances the Wolvertons wouldn't bother them anymore with cops around, but then she remembered what Julie had said about that bunch having friends on the force.

She wondered if the newcomer would be neutral, a friend . . . or an enemy.

She wouldn't have to wait long to find out. A minute or so later, a man came through the café door wearing brown uniform trousers, a short-sleeved khaki shirt with a badge pinned to it, dark sunglasses, and a dark brown Stetson on graying, sandy hair. The gunbelt around his lean waist had an attached holster with a black semi-automatic pistol in it, as well as pouches that contained a taser and a radio.

The man took off his sunglasses as he walked up to the counter. His gaze flicked around the room, and Callie had a feeling he didn't miss much. Without the glasses covering his eyes, the man's craggy features didn't appear quite so menacing.

She saw that his glance lingered longer on her, Joseph, and Julie than it did on anyone else in the café. Of course he would notice them. She and Joseph were strangers, and evidently he hadn't expected to see Julie here.

"Hello, Froggy," he greeted the proprietor as he hung the sunglasses by one leg in the breast pocket of his uniform shirt.

"Evening, Sheriff," Froggy replied. "Coffee?"

"Of course."

Froggy filled a thick, white ceramic mug from the spout on a tall, stainless-steel coffee urn. He put it on the counter in front of the lawman, who stood behind the empty stool to Joseph's right but made no move to sit down. Callie noticed that he reached for the mug with his left hand. His right wasn't far from the butt of the holstered pistol.

The sheriff took a sip, nodded and said to Froggy, "Good as always."

"Thanks, Sheriff."

The lawman turned his head a little and said, "Hello, Julie. How's your grandfather doing?"

"Not bad, Sheriff, thank you," she said. "At least he was a couple of days ago. That's the last time I got by Sleepy Pines to check on him."

"Well, next time you see him, give him my best."

"I sure will, Sheriff," Julie said.

"How about your daddy? Seen him lately?"

Julie frowned. "You know better than that. My daddy's nowhere in this part of the country."

"That's what people keep telling me," the sheriff said, nodding slowly. "But somehow I just can't see ol' Larry Don being able to stay away from this neck of the woods for too long."

Callie forced herself to keep an expression of mild, polite interest on her face, as if she were listening to a conversation about people she had never heard of before. She glanced at Joseph and saw that he was doing the same.

So Julie was Larry Don Barlow's daughter. It was a wild coincidence that she and Joseph had come along just in time to save the daughter of the man they were looking for from a couple of fellas who obviously had bad intentions. But wild coincidences drove a bigger part of life than most people ever thought about, she mused. In many respects, life itself was a wild coincidence, if you stopped to ponder it long enough.

The sheriff finally decided to acknowledge the presence of strangers in their midst. He took another sip of coffee, then turned and extended his right hand to Joseph.

"Sheriff Howard Whitfield," he introduced himself.

"Joseph Kingfisher." Joseph clasped the lawman's hand. "And this is my sister Callie."

Whitfield took a step back and reached behind Julie to shake Callie's hand as she turned halfway on the stool. "Ms. Kingfisher," he said. "Or do you maybe have a married name?"

"No. Callie will do."

In her experience, most guys were flirting and trying to find out if she had a husband when they asked something like that. But not Sheriff Howard Whitfield, she sensed. He was looking for information, all right, but for its own sake, not because he had any other interest in her. He just wanted to know who was in his county.

To further that, he asked, "What brings you folks to Hackberry County?"

"I have a question," Callie said, not answering his. "Why are the town and the county called Hackberry when, clearly, we're surrounded by pine trees?"

Whitfield smiled. "The fellas who came up with that name a hundred and fifty years ago weren't exactly botanists. But, if you look, there are other trees besides pines that grow around here. We have quite a few hackberry trees growing in these parts, mostly along the creeks. Maybe those fellas knew what they were doing, after all."

"I suppose so."

The sheriff's smile didn't go away, but his voice was a little stiffer as he went on, "And don't think I didn't notice that you avoided my question, Ms. Kingfisher."

Joseph said, "There's nothing suspicious about it, Sheriff. My sister was just indulging her curiosity, that's all. We're here to check out one of your local retirement homes." He nodded to Julie. "I believe you mentioned it, Miss Barlow. Sleepy Pines."

"That's where my granddaddy lives," she said. "That's really why you're here?"

"That's right," Callie said. "We're looking for a nice place for *our* grandfather." She put a concerned look on her face. "He really doesn't need to be living by himself anymore, since our grandmother passed away last year. But he has such a fierce streak of independence, we're having a hard time convincing him he'd be better off someplace nice, where he could be taken care of."

"But if you're not from around here," Whitfield said, "what made you think about moving him into Sleepy Pines?"

"Granddad lived in East Texas when he was a boy," Joseph answered, just as promptly and smoothly as if he'd been telling the truth, "and has always said that he'd like to come back to the Piney Woods someday."

"We did some research, and this Sleepy Pines Retirement Home is rated pretty highly," Callie said, picking up the story. "And it seemed worth the drive to check it out." She smiled. "Besides, it's lovely here."

"If you like trees," Froggy said from the other side of the counter. "Because that's what we've got more of than anything else."

Whitfield looked at them for a second and then gave them another of those slow, deliberate nods. "I see. I wasn't aware that Sleepy Pines had such a good reputation. But I'll admit, I don't keep up with such things. And I don't remember the last time we had to answer a call to the rest home. They have a pretty peaceful bunch there."

Joseph actually had looked up Sleepy Pines Retirement Home, Callie knew, since it was going to be the starting point in their search for Larry Don Barlow. It rated only average as a retirement home, he had said, but there were no red flags about it to serve as warnings to the families of potential residents. So their cover story was plausible enough.

Of course, neither of them could have predicted that they would run into Barlow's daughter before they ever reached the town of Hackberry.

"Peaceful is good," Joseph said. "When you get to a certain age, I suppose that's what you crave more than anything else: peace and quiet."

"You seem to have plenty of that around here," Callie added. "You've got the Lazy Pines Motel and the Sleepy Pines Retirement Home . . ."

"And the Slumbering Pines Lodge, on up the road," Froggy said. He dropped an eyelid in a wink. "My competition."

"We like to take it easy, all right," Whitfield said. He drank the last of the coffee and placed the empty cup on the counter without ever sitting down, which sort of belied his words. "Thanks, Froggy. Put it on my tab."

"Will do, Sheriff. Say, I thought maybe you could run Julie home—"

Julie interrupted him by saying, "That's all right, Sheriff, you don't need to do that. I told Callie and Joseph earlier that I'd show them where Sleepy Pines is, and while we're there, I'll pop in and say hello to Granddaddy Seth."

"I see," Whitfield said. "Sounds like you have a plan all worked out, then." He nodded to Joseph and Callie. "You folks enjoy your stay in Hackberry."

Whitfield left the café and got back in his SUV. Froggy watched him go, then said, "You didn't say anything to the sheriff about that run-in with the Wolvertons. He could've gone and had a talk with them."

"It wouldn't do any good." Julie's voice hardened as she added, "Besides, you know we like to keep some things private, Froggy."

The white-haired man grunted. "I've been around here a heck of a lot longer than you have, girl. I know how things work in Hackberry County, all right." He looked at Callie and Joseph. "But you two are strangers and don't know our ways. You want to walk careful around here and not get mixed up in things that don't concern you."

"We're not looking for trouble—" Joseph began.

"There won't be any," Julie broke in. "By now, the Wolvertons will have driven by here looking for us and seen the sheriff's SUV out there. For all they know, we reported what happened to Sheriff Whitfield. They'll head back into the woods and lie low for a while, just in case."

Froggy shrugged. "More than likely."

"Anyway, I really would like to show you where the rest home is and introduce you to the folks there," Julie said to Callie and Joseph. "After you helped me, it's the least I can do."

"We appreciate that," Callie said.

And while Julie was doing that, maybe she would drop some clue as to where her daddy was. Not likely, maybe, but the possibility couldn't be ruled out.

As they were about to leave, Froggy asked, "You want me to hold a couple of cabins for you folks, in case you decide to come back here and spend the night?"

"We'll probably stay in town," Joseph said.

"Suit yourself. But you're always welcome at the Lazy Pines."

"We'll remember that," Callie said. "Thank you."

"Sure thing. Y'all come back now, hear?"

Callie looked around as they left the café. She didn't see the big work truck or any motorcycles anywhere around. But with the trees being so thick, it was hard to see very far in any direction.

"You really don't have to show us where the rest home is," Joseph said to Julie as they all climbed into the Ram. "We can just take you home, if you want to tell us how to get there."

"No, I don't mind at all," she insisted. "Besides, I really ought to stop in and see my granddaddy for a few minutes. We try to check on him every day or two."

"That's good of you to be so devoted like that," Callie said as Joseph pulled out onto the highway and headed toward Hackberry again.

"My daddy says that folks these days don't respect their elders enough, the way they used to."

Callie smiled over the seat. "He's probably right about that."

"He's right about a lot of things. I never saw anybody better at sizing folks up, and he tried to teach me how to do that, too." Julie's voice changed as she went on, "That's how I know that everything you told Sheriff Whitfield back there was a pack of lies, and why I want to know what you're really doing in Hackberry County."

CHAPTER 10

Callie turned more to frown back at the young woman.

"That's not a very nice thing to say after we helped you like we did," she said. "You just called us liars."

"I'm sorry," Julie said. She sounded like she really meant it. "But I know a crock of bull when I hear it, and that's what you told the sheriff. Besides, the way Mr. Kingfisher drove when they were chasing us, and then shot out the windshield of the Wolvertons' truck . . . it was like you're a spy or something, Mr. Kingfisher!"

"Well . . . spies can have grandfathers who need to go to retirement homes, can't they?" Joseph asked. Callie could tell he was trying to keep his tone light, but she wasn't sure how well he succeeded.

Not well enough to fool Julie. "Is that it?" she asked, completely serious. "Are you a spy?" She looked at Callie. "Both of you?" Then her eyebrows went up and she continued, "I'll bet you're not even brother and sister! You're spies . . . and lovers—"

"Hold it, hold it," Callie interrupted her. "We're definitely brother and sister. In fact, we're twins." She left it at that, rather than explaining that they had begun life as triplets. "Joey's my little brother by five minutes."

Without taking his eyes off the road, Joseph said, "Five minutes isn't long enough for you to call me your little brother, *Callista.*"

"Oh, shut up."

Julie looked a little more uncertain than she had a moment earlier. Their banter certainly sounded like that of siblings. She said, "What about the way you carry a gun and are so good with it?"

"I go to the range and practice a lot," Joseph said. "And there's nothing unusual about somebody carrying a gun. These days, most places you go, some of the people are armed, whether you know it or not."

Callie thought about mentioning that she was carrying. During the chase earlier, she had thought about pulling the Shield Joseph had loaned her, but she hadn't figured it would do any good. It had taken Joseph's quick wits to come up with a workable plan, although she hated to admit that, even to herself.

She didn't believe it would help matters at the moment to mention the gun in the belly holster she wore, so she kept that to herself. Julie already looked doubtful about the suspicions she had expressed; let it stay that way, Callie decided.

"I'm not sure I believe y'all," Julie said with a frown, "but I guess if you really *were* spies, you wouldn't be allowed to tell me." She sighed. "And I don't suppose it really matters. You saved me from the Wolvertons, and that's what counts. I'm mighty grateful for that."

"Just who *are* these Wolvertons, anyway?" Callie asked.

"A bunch of sorry, no-good sons of—" Julie began with heat in her voice. She stopped short, drew in a breath through her nose, and went on, "My mama fought a losing battle to teach me how to be ladylike, but I guess out of respect for her memory I shouldn't do a bunch of cussin'. Let's just say that my family and the Wolvertons don't get along, and that goes 'way back."

"A feud," Callie said. "Like the Hatfields and the McCoys."

Julie shrugged. "Something like that."

Callie figured there was more to it, but she didn't want to push too hard. Instead she said, "They sound like a bad bunch."

"The worst." Julie hesitated, then went on, "I'll be honest with you, since you helped me and all. The Barlows don't have the greatest reputation around these parts. But the Wolvertons are worse. Lots worse."

Joseph said, "From what I've seen, I can believe it. The fellows in that truck came very close to killing us."

"That's what they aimed to do," Julie said flatly.

"Earl and Norman," Callie said. "That's what Froggy called them, isn't it?"

Julie nodded. "Yeah."

"Brothers to Tom and Jimmy?"

"Cousins. Old Enoch Wolverton had five sons, and they all had a bunch of kids. There are Wolvertons spread all over the county."

"What about your family?" Joseph asked. "How big is it?"

"Big . . . but not as big as the Wolvertons. Granddaddy Seth and Grandma Eloise had four kids, two boys and two girls, and none of them spawned offspring as fast as the Wolvertons did." Julie laughed. "Spawned offspring. You hear that? That's the way my granddaddy talks half the time, like he was reading from the Bible or Shakespeare or something. I guess maybe some of it's rubbed off on me."

"I think I'd like to meet your grandfather," Callie said.

"I'll introduce you when we stop at Sleepy Pines. I warn you, though. He's still got an eye for the ladies. As pretty as you are, he'll flirt shamelessly, Ms. Kingfisher."

"Callie."

"You just keep an eye on his hands, if you know what's good for you, Callie."

Apparently casual, Joseph said, "Did the sheriff say your father was out of town, Julie?"

"That's right. He's off working. In, uh, West Texas. Oil and gas."

Julie was young enough that she wasn't completely smooth with her lies.

"You live with your mother?" Callie asked.

"That's right. And my little brother and sister."

"After we're done at the rest home, we can drop you off there, if you'd like," Joseph said.

"Y'all don't have to go to that much trouble."

"It wouldn't be any bother," Callie said.

"We'll see." Julie pointed over the seat. "We're fixing to get into town."

Callie had already spotted the old-fashioned water tower, perched high on four legs overlooking the town. A moment later she was able to see several church steeples and the tall roofs on which they sat. The trees began to thin out considerably as the pickup reached the outskirts of town. Residences lined both sides of the road. Trees had been cut down so that those houses could be built, but each yard seemed to have at least a couple of towering pines left in it. The same was true on the side streets they passed.

Callie saw two red lights ahead. Hackberry's business district was three blocks long, lined with brick and rock buildings and an occasional, older-looking frame structure.

"You just keep going straight ahead," Julie told Joseph. "Sleepy Pines is on the other side of town."

The first red light marked the intersection of another state highway. A drugstore, a bank, a title company, and a meat market were located on the four corners. Business buildings extended a block in both directions. The same was true at the next light, where the cross street was just a local one, but also lined with businesses for a block. Hackberry looked like a nice little town, the sort of peaceful community that could be found all over Texas once you got out of the big cities.

Not that it was without its problems, Callie thought. They probably had issues with crime and drugs here, just like anywhere else. The deep woods around the town were prime locations for old mobile homes being used as meth labs, she figured. But to somebody just passing through, Hackberry would look more like Mayberry.

They passed a large building on the left that Julie pointed

out as the local soft drink bottling plant. Just beyond it was a barn-like wooden structure that appeared to be abandoned. Train tracks running next to it crossed the highway, but there were no signals.

"The train doesn't run through here anymore," Julie offered by way of explanation without being asked as the pickup rattled over the tracks. "That hurt business quite a bit, and the town hasn't really recovered from it yet."

"I didn't see too many empty buildings as we came through downtown," Callie commented. "Looks like most of the businesses are still trying to make a go of it."

"We're stubborn around here."

They passed a Dairy Queen on the other side of the road, then a Mexican restaurant. Neither place was crowded, but some customers were there.

Julie pointed and told Joseph, "Turn right up here at the next street."

He did so. On the left was a sprawling, one-story building with a hedge-lined circle drive in front of it. A couple of wings extended back from the ends of the building. It formed a U-shape like the Lazy Pines Motel, although this was all one building, not a collection of cabins, and the open end faced away from the street, not toward it.

A sign on the lawn inside the circle drive read *SLEEPY PINES RETIREMENT HOME*. Below the name in smaller letters was *Where You and Your Loved Ones Can Take It Easy*.

"Go past and park in the lot on the other side," Julie said. "That drive in the front is where residents are unloaded. And sometimes loaded."

Callie glanced back at her with a puzzled look.

"When the funeral home comes to pick them up," Julie explained.

"Oh." Callie shook her head. "I guess that does happen now and then in a place like this, doesn't it?"

"Pretty often, really," Julie said matter-of-factly. "Most folks, by the time their families get them in a rest home, they don't last more than a few months. There are always some exceptions, of course. My granddaddy's been here almost two years. And there's one lady who's been here for five years." A worried expression crossed her face. "That doesn't mean that y'all's grandfather won't last very long if he comes here. I didn't mean to suggest that."

"Don't worry," Callie assured her. "Our grandfather is in pretty good shape for his age."

She felt a little bad about maintaining that fiction. Julie seemed like a nice young woman and Callie didn't like lying to her. But Julie's father was a criminal who had skipped out on his bail, she reminded herself, and it was her and Joseph's job to find him and take him back to Corpus Christi. Like it or not, Julie was just a possible means to that end.

While they were talking, Joseph had turned left into an asphalt-paved parking lot that ran alongside the other wing of the rest home. He piloted the pickup into an empty space between a Jeep and a Toyota sedan.

As they followed a sidewalk around to the front of the building, Julie said, "I was wondering, Callie . . . I don't mean to pry, but how'd you hurt your leg?"

"I had a fall a while back." That much was the truth,

anyway. "Broke a bone. But I had good doctors and it's healing up just fine. Practically healed, in fact. I just use this cane because the leg starts to get a little tired and sore if I'm on it too much."

"Oh. I'm sorry to hear you got hurt. You look like a real athlete."

"She was," Joseph said. "Callie was always incredibly good at sports." He cleared his throat. "I was the more bookish sibling."

"Well, being smart is worth something, too." Julie added hastily to Callie, "Not that I'm saying you're not smart—"

Callie laughed. "I know what you meant. Again, don't worry about it."

Joseph reached the glass doors first and held the one on the right open. The three of them stepped into the cool, disinfectant-smelling air of the Sleepy Pines Retirement Home.

Chapter 11

A large area that looked like the living room in someone's house opened to the right. Carpet with a very short nap covered the floor. Some potted plants were scattered around, along with heavily upholstered armchairs and sofas, and some straight-backed chairs, as well. A couple of polished wooden tables sat on one side of the room. A partially completed jigsaw puzzle was laid out on one table, while a set of dominoes had been turned face-down and pushed into the center of the other table, ready to be shuffled for the next hand of Forty-Two. No one was sitting at either table.

Directly in front of the entrance doors was an arched opening that led into a good-sized dining room. At least two dozen residents were spread out among the tables, eating their supper. It didn't really seem late enough for that, Callie thought, but she reminded herself that elderly people often liked to eat early, so they could turn in early.

To the left was a counter, and behind it an office area with several desks. A middle-aged woman with short, curly, graying brown hair stood behind the counter and greeted Julie by name.

"I didn't expect to see you this late in the day, honey," she said.

"I happened to be in the neighborhood," Julie said, which wasn't exactly true, "and I thought I'd stop in and say hello to Granddaddy. I didn't see him in the dining room, though."

"He's feelin' a little under the weather, so he's havin' supper in his room this evening." The woman looked at Joseph and Callie. "Who are your friends?"

"This is, uh, Joseph and Callie Kingfisher. I met them earlier today, and they said they wanted to see if they thought their grandfather would like it here."

That put a professional smile on the woman's face. "Well, I'm certainly glad to meet you, Mr. and Mrs. Kingfisher. I'm Donna Giddings, the director of Sleepy Pines. It's a little later than we usually give tours to prospective clients, but if you'd like to take a look around . . ."

"Thank you, Ms. Giddings," Joseph said. "By the way, Callie is my sister, not my wife."

"Oh, I'm sorry. I meant no offense—"

"None taken," Callie assured her. "Actually, Julie here offered to introduce us to her grandfather. We thought we'd talk to him and find out how he likes it here. But if he's not feeling well . . ."

"No, no, Seth loves visitors. He'll perk right up when he sees you. You just feel free to look around, though." A faintly disapproving expression came over Donna Giddings' face. "Some places don't like people poking around, but we have nothing to hide here at Sleepy Pines."

Callie wasn't sure if that was a hundred percent true—everybody had *something* they'd just as soon nobody else knew about—but the woman sounded sincere.

To the left of the dining room was a hallway that led down the wing on that side. With Julie a step in front of them to show the way, Callie and Joseph followed her. The floors were tile here, a neutral gray color that wouldn't show dirt, and the walls were painted a soothing light yellow. Numbered doors were on both sides of the corridor. Framed prints hung on the walls, all landscapes, some paintings and some photographs.

Julie stopped in front of a door with a number 8 tacked to it. She knocked lightly, twisted the handle, and called, "Granddaddy, it's me," as she opened the door a little.

"Julie?" The man's voice had a hint of an old age quaver to it but was still fairly strong. "Come on in, girl."

Julie pushed the door back the rest of the way and stepped into the room with Callie and Joseph behind her. She said, "I brought some friends of mine with me, Granddaddy. I hope that's all right."

A man sat in an armchair near the window with a folding table in front of him. His supper dishes and a glass of iced tea were on a tray sitting on that table. He wore a t-shirt with a cartoon fisherman on it, and over that a plaid flannel shirt. Legs in gray sweat pants stuck out from under the table and ended in fuzzy houseshoes.

Despite the old man's garb, Seth Barlow was still a pretty formidable figure, Callie realized. His shoulders were broad, and although there was a bit of a gut under the barrel chest, he appeared solidly built. He had a fringe of white hair around a mostly bald head, and a thick white mustache drooped over his lips and past the corners of his mouth. His dark-eyed gaze fastened on the visitors through thick-lensed glasses.

"Good Lord, girl!" he said. "You brought John Law in here?"

"No, no," Julie said as she waved a hand at her two companions. "This is Callie and Joseph Kingfisher. They helped me out earlier today, and since they're looking for a place for their grandfather, I brought them with me to show them Sleepy Pines."

"They're lyin' to you." Barlow pushed the table back so he could sit forward. He pointed a gnarled finger at Joseph and went on, "That one's a cop. I can smell it on him."

Joseph smiled, shook his head, and said, "You're mistaken, Mr. Barlow. I'm not a police officer."

Julie frowned at him. "You know, in all the excitement, I never did find out what you really do." She glanced at her grandfather. "I accused him earlier of being a spy."

"He's no spy," Barlow said darkly. "John Law, that's what he is."

Joseph shook his head. "I'm sorry, but you're mistaken, sir. I work with computers."

That was true . . . sort of, Callie thought.

The old man's gaze darted over to her. "What about her?"

"She can speak for herself, thank you," Callie said. "I'm in the movie business. I work in Hollywood."

Julie's eyes widened. "Really?"

Callie gave a little shake of her head and said, "All behind the scenes stuff." That was a lie, but she certainly wasn't famous and didn't like pretending to be.

"Are you sure? Now that I think about it, you do look a little like a movie star."

Callie supposed that was true. She looked a little like a number of different movie stars, which was why she could double for them when it came time to shoot the dangerous stuff. At least, that's what she'd been doing for quite a while. As things stood now, she didn't know when she'd get back to that.

"Anyway, they really helped me out earlier today, Granddaddy, and I trust them," Julie went on. "So I wish you'd be polite to them."

"You're too trustin' for your own good," Barlow muttered. "All you youngsters are. You don't know how the world's just layin' in wait, ready to jump you and gut you like a fish when you're least expectin' it."

"Well, if you're going to be like that, maybe we should just go—"

"No, no," Barlow said, lifting a hand to motion them closer. "Come on in and shut the door. Sorry for bein' unfriendly. I'm just a cantankerous old coot sometimes." He put his hands on the arms of the chair and pushed himself to his feet, then extended a hand to Joseph. "Seth Barlow. Nice to meetcha."

"Joseph Kingfisher," Joseph said as he shook hands. "This is my sister Callie."

"Sister? I figured you two was hitched."

Callie rolled her eyes. "I don't know why everybody seems to think that."

"They're twins," Julie put in.

Barlow squinted at Callie, then looked at Joseph. "Yeah, I can see that a little," he admitted. He summoned up a smile for Callie. "My apologies, Miss Kingfisher. My faculties must have been a trifle discombobulated. It's not often that such a rare beauty as yourself deigns to pay me a visit."

"See, I told you he talks weird sometimes," Julie said.

"Because I speak English and don't communicate in abbreviations and initials and emojicons like you young people?" Barlow snorted. "I may be just an ignorant backwoods ridgerunner in a lot of ways, but I always had a head for reading." He waved a hand again. "Sit down, sit down." He patted the arm of the chair as he lowered himself into it again. "You can perch right here if you want, Miss Kingfisher."

Julie said, "No, you and Joseph take those straight chairs there, and I'll sit on the bed. Granddaddy, you go ahead and finish your supper while we talk."

"I've had enough of it," Barlow said, shaking his head. "Don't get me wrong, the food here is good, but I just don't have much appetite these days."

"I'm sorry to hear that," Callie said as she took one of the straight-backed chairs Julie had indicated.

"Don't be. Time wounds all heels. Age catches up to the best of us." The old man sighed. "So you're thinking about putting your grandfather in here?"

"That's right," Joseph said. "Is it a good establishment?"

"Good as any, I suppose. Like I said, the food's not bad. And the place is clean. That's not something you find in every retirement home. Donna—Ms Giddings—she runs a pretty tight ship. Doesn't put up with employees who slack off and neglect the residents. Speaking of which, the residents aren't a bad bunch. Not that I get all friendly with any of them." Barlow blew out a breath. "That'd just be a waste of time."

"Granddaddy!" Julie scolded.

"Well? It's the truth." He looked at Joseph and Callie again. "What kind of shape is your grandfather in? Is he still a fairly active man?"

"I suppose you could say so," Joseph said.

"There's not much to do here, but there's a little shuffle-board court out back." Barlow chuckled. "That tells you how long ago it's been that this place was built. Old folks still played shuffleboard back then."

"Are they good about letting family visit?"

"Oh, sure. My kids and *their* kids are in and out of here pretty often."

Callie said, "You must miss your son . . . Julie's father, I mean . . . since she said he's off working in another part of the state."

Barlow didn't miss a beat. He shrugged and said, "Ah, Larry Don'll be back. Can't blame the boy for going where the work is. He's always been the industrious sort."

Callie just nodded and didn't look at Joseph. Either Seth Barlow didn't know that his son was a fugitive—which seemed unlikely—or else he was used to covering for Larry Don.

Callie wondered just how much of a family business crime was for the Barlows.

CHAPTER 12

After they had chatted inconsequentially for a few more minutes, Julie said, "We'd better go on and let you get your rest, Granddaddy."

Barlow turned his head to glance out the window. "It's not even dark yet," he said. "The sun's not down."

"No, but Callie and Joseph have been on the road most of the day, and I'm sure they'd like to find a place to stay. I thought I'd help them."

"Take them to the Lodge," Barlow said.

Julie nodded. "That's what I figured."

"The Slumbering Pines Lodge?" Callie said.

Barlow looked a little surprised. "You've heard of it?"

"Somebody mentioned it." Julie hadn't told her grandfather anything about the trouble with the Wolvertons or the stop they had made at Froggy's, and if she wanted to keep that from him, Callie was willing to go along with it for now.

"Some friends of ours run the place," Barlow said. "Julie will get you a good deal."

"We appreciate that," Joseph said.

"If you decide to put your grandfather here, bring him by and introduce me to the old coot."

"Granddaddy!" From the sound of it, Julie was used to admonishing her grandfather for his plain-spoken ways.

"Honey, *everybody's* an old coot if they live long enough," he said. He stood up, shook hands with Joseph again, and then took Callie's hand in both of his. "And of course, you're welcome to stop by any time, Miss Kingfisher. Day or night."

"I don't know about that," Callie told him with a smile. "I'm not sure I'd want to visit without a chaperone."

"Why, you don't need a chaperone with me! I'm just a harmless old man."

"I'll think about it."

"I'll hold you to that."

Julie hugged her grandfather, then ushered Callie and Joseph out of the room and back toward the entrance.

"I warned you about him," she said quietly. "He's . . . what's the word?"

"Incorrigible?" Callie suggested.

"More like randy as an old goat." Julie smiled and shook her head. "But I guess that shows he's still alive and k-kicking."

The slight catch in her voice made Callie look over at her.

"He has stomach cancer," Julie said, so quietly that Callie almost couldn't make out the words. "After the last round of tests, the doctor said he might last another six months."

"I'm sorry," Joseph said. "Honestly, he doesn't seem like he's in such bad shape."

"He doesn't let anybody see how much he's hurting, not if he can help it. The family can see a difference in him. Most other folks can't."

"I'm really sorry," Callie said. "I like him. He's . . . a character."

"He is that," Julie agreed. She managed to smile. "But let's go on out to the Lodge and see if we can get you two settled in. I'm sure you're tired."

"It *has* been a long day," Joseph said.

That was true. Callie had a hard time believing that they had been in Corpus Christi only that morning. An awful lot had happened since then.

Back in the pickup once more, Julie gave them directions to the Slumbering Pines Lodge, which was another quarter of a mile out the highway, on the other side of the road. Like the Lazy Pines on the other side of town, the motel had a rustic look to it, although it seemed to be of slightly more recent vintage than its competition. Probably built in the Sixties instead of the Fifties, Callie decided. It was a two-story L, with the short side on the back and the office at the front of the long side. Across the parking lot was a separate building with a sign on the roof that read *COFFEE SHOP.*

Julie told Joseph to park in front of the office. They went inside and found a tall, slender, brown-haired man behind the counter. He wore glasses and had a nervous manner, but the smile with which he greeted them was friendly enough.

"Howdy, Julie," he said. "Haven't seen you around in a while."

"Oh, I've been around," she told him. "Dennis, these are

friends of mine. Callie and Joseph Kingfisher. They're brother and sister, not a married couple."

"Well, I wasn't gonna assume anything. Fact of the matter is, I knew right off that you two were related by blood." The words came out in a sly drawl. "Twins, aren't you?"

"That's right," Callie said. "Not many people recognize that right away."

"Oh, I make it a habit to study folks' faces, ma'am. Running a motel, you know, I see so many people come through here, and they're all different and all interesting, you know? Everybody has a different story. By the way, I'm Dennis Ordway. My wife and I run the lodge. My wife is Julie's cousin."

"Shirttail cousin," Julie said.

"Now, I've never really understood that term," Ordway said. "All I know is, we're kin, and if you folks are friends of Julie's, that entitles you to the friends and family discount, yes, it does. I just need a driver's license and a credit card . . ."

Joseph provided both of those things and quickly completed checking in, asking Ordway for two single rooms.

"I'll put you in Eleven and Twelve," the man said. "They're down there in the wing on the end, farthest from the road. Nice and quiet. Of course, the trees come right up behind those units, so you might hear some things moving around in the woods, but the traffic noise won't bother you, no, sir."

"Thanks," Joseph said, although he sounded a little unsure about what Ordway had meant by that.

Callie said to Julie, "And now we need to run you home before it gets any later."

"That's all right," the young woman said. "You don't have

to do that. I can get home from here. It's not that far."

"But you've been so helpful to us," Joseph said. "It's the least we can do."

Julie shook her head. "It's really not necessary."

Despite both Callie and Joseph protesting that it was no trouble, Julie insisted on not bothering them. Callie wondered if she was actually just being careful and not letting them know where she lived. Maybe Seth Barlow's suspicions had gotten through to his granddaughter after all.

They left the office and paused beside the pickup. "Don't worry about Dennis," Julie said. "He comes across as a little creepy sometimes, but he's harmless. And Belinda, his wife, is just as sweet as she can be."

Callie tried one more time. "Are you sure you don't want us to take you home?"

"I'm sure. It's not far."

"What about the Wolvertons?" Joseph asked.

"I'm not worried about them. They won't try anything this close to town. Anyway, after that run-in with you two, they'll be licking their wounds for a while. They'll lie low."

"If you're sure," Callie said. Pushing the matter too far seemed unwise to her, even though she wasn't a detective. Joseph didn't seem to disagree.

Joseph had picked up one of the travel brochures in a display on the counter inside the office. Now he took a pen from his pocket and wrote on it before handing it to Julie.

"That's my cell phone number. If you need any help while we're in town, call me."

Julie narrowed her eyes at him. "Are you sure you're not a

spy? Because that sounds kind of like something a spy would say."

"Not at all. But I've run into troublemakers like the Wolvertons before. They're not the type to get hit and not hit back."

"Well, that's true, I suppose." Julie nodded. "Thank you, both of you, for your help today. That business with Tom and Jimmy . . . well, it could have ended pretty bad if y'all hadn't come along when you did. I'd give you my cell phone number, but I lost the blasted thing out there in the woods. Probably never see it again. If you need to get in touch with me, though, you know where to find Granddaddy. He can always get word to me."

"Thanks." Callie smiled. "I hope we see you again before we leave."

"I do, too." Impulsively, Julie gave her a hug and then shook hands with Joseph. "I'll be seeing y'all."

She started walking toward the road. Quietly, Joseph said to Callie, "We might as well go put our bags in the rooms."

"Yeah, I suppose so." Once they were in the pickup, she added, "I know we have Larry Don's address, but I kind of wanted to see the place."

"We'll find it," Joseph said confidently as he pulled the pickup through the lot, back to the lodge's short rear wing.

"Dennis there in the office really was kind of creepy," Callie said. "What did he mean by saying we might hear things in the woods? What sort of things are *in* those woods, anyway?"

"I'd just as soon not find out," Joseph said.

◆ ◊ ◆

Outside, the motel might look like it was stuck in the Six-ties, but inside the rooms, it was obvious that many remodel-ings had been carried out since then, Callie discovered when she looked around. The bed was comfortable, and there was an equally comfortable armchair. A small desk on one side of the room had an office chair in front of it and a laminated piece of paper with instructions for how to access the lodge's free wi-fi. A decent-sized flatscreen TV hung on the wall above a dresser with several drawers in it. On top of the dresser was another laminated guide listing all the cable TV channels available.

"Everything's up to date in Hackberry," Callie muttered as she set her bag and her small rolling suitcase on the bed.

She unpacked quickly and hung up her clothes, put her makeup bag and other personal things in the bathroom, and had just come out of there when someone knocked on the door. She went over and opened it, expecting to see Joseph. They had agreed earlier that they would have supper in the coffee shop across the parking lot. It had been a long day, and that was the simplest, easiest thing to do.

Instead of her brother, Sheriff Howard Whitfield stood there. He had taken off his sunglasses already and hung them in his shirt pocket.

"Hello, Sheriff. I didn't expect to see you again so soon." Or at all, if she was being honest, Callie thought. Although, now that she considered it, she supposed that given the job that had brought her and Joseph here, it was likely they would have been interacting with local law enforcement at some point.

"Well, I happened to be passing by and wanted to talk to you and your brother again for a few minutes," Whitfield replied. "Dennis up at the office told me you had Rooms Eleven and Twelve, but I wasn't sure which of you was in which room."

"How did you even know we were staying here?"

Whitfield smiled. "Not that many places to stay in Hackberry. Plus I spotted your pickup." He nodded toward the Ram. "Not that many California license plates around here, either."

"I suppose not," Callie said, although with all the people who had moved from California to Texas in the past couple of decades, she would have thought that California plates wouldn't be *that* rare.

Whitfield leaned his head toward the next room. "You think we could go next door and get your brother in on this conversation?"

"That depends. Just what is it you want to know, Sheriff?"

The smile remained on Whitfield's face, but his voice took on a slightly harder edge as he said, "I'd like to know what it is that brings a private eye from Corpus Christi and his movie star sister to our little wide place in the road."

CHAPTER 13

Callie was surprised, but she tried not to let it show on her face. Instead, she laughed and said, "I don't know where you got that information, but you've been misinformed."

"Oh? How's that?"

"I'm a far cry from a movie star."

"You have your own IMDB page," he pointed out.

"So does practically everybody else who ever stepped foot on a movie set," she said. "That doesn't make me a movie star."

He shrugged. "Maybe not in your opinion. But you've been in a bunch of movies and worked with some really big names, so folks around here would consider you a star. And I notice you didn't deny what I said about your brother being a private detective."

"Let me guess," Callie said. "After meeting us at Froggy's, you looked us up."

"I like to know who's in my county. And, being in law enforcement, I have access to quite a few sources of information.

Although this day and age, anybody who knows much of anything about computers can find out all sorts of things in not much time at all."

He was right about that. Not much in life was secret anymore.

But evidently he didn't know they were here in search of Larry Don Barlow. Callie wasn't sure what to tell him. She didn't know if he was an ally of the Barlow family, an enemy, or strictly neutral. As a lawman, he ought to be somebody that she and Joseph could turn to for help, but they had no guarantee of that being true.

She didn't have to stand there filled with uncertainty for long, because at that moment, the door of the next room opened and Joseph stepped out. He stopped short at the sight of Callie and Whitfield standing in front of the open door of Room Twelve.

Joseph recovered almost instantly, of course. It was hard to throw him for a loop for very long. He said, "Hello again, Sheriff. Were you looking for me?"

"Both of you, actually, Mr. Kingfisher, so I'm glad you're here. Can we step inside one of the rooms and talk for a minute?"

"If we say no," Callie said, "is the next move to take us down to the station?"

That brought a laugh from Whitfield. He said, "I can sure tell that you've worked a lot in the movies, Ms. Kingfisher. That's just the sort of thing those Hollywood scriptwriters would come up with, isn't it?"

Joseph said, "Why don't you come in, Sheriff? We have

nothing to hide."

Whitfield walked toward him, saying, "That's good. I'm glad to hear that."

Joseph motioned for Callie to come along. The three of them went in Joseph's room, which was laid out and furnished identically to Callie's. He shut the door and said, "I'd offer you something to drink, Sheriff, but there isn't anything. I haven't even visited the ice machine yet."

Whitfield waved that off. "No, no, that's fine. Thank you anyway."

"That armchair looks to be the most comfortable. Why don't you have a seat?"

Whitfield took off his hat and sat down in the chair. Joseph turned around the chair at the desk and took a seat on it, and Callie perched on the edge of the bed.

"What can we do for you?" Joseph asked.

Whitfield countered with a question of his own. "Julie Barlow get home all right?"

"I suppose so. She came here with us and helped us get checked in, then insisted that she could walk home on her own. We told her we didn't mind taking her, but she said she would be fine." Joseph shrugged. "It didn't seem like it was our place to argue with her."

"You wouldn't have gotten very far if you had. Julie's like all the other Barlows. She's got a mind of her own. They're a stubborn bunch." Whitfield toyed idly with his hat, which he had balanced on his knee, and went on, "Not the friendliest bunch, either. In fact, to be honest I'm surprised she took up with a couple of strangers like you folks. No offense, of course."

"None taken. We *are* strangers."

"From Corpus Christi." Whitfield looked at Callie. "And Hollywood."

"So you know who we are," Joseph said.

"He does," Callie said. "And what we are."

Joseph looked for a second as if he might be considering denying it, but then he shrugged in acceptance.

"All right, Sheriff. Say what you came to say."

"You know, some might consider it professional courtesy for a private investigator to check in with the local authorities when he comes into a new town on a job."

"I haven't said that I'm here on a case," Joseph pointed out.

"Well, I'm pretty sure you and your sister aren't sight-seeing, and that story about looking for a retirement home for your grandfather . . . that's just a story, and not one that I put much stock in, right from the start." Whitfield pursed his lips and shook his head. "No, the only reason I can see for you to be here in Hackberry, Mr. Kingfisher, is that you're looking for Larry Don Barlow."

So he *had* figured it out, after all.

"But why you brought your sister along, now *that* is a mystery to me," Whitfield went on.

Joseph shook his head. "I know Larry Don Barlow is Julie's father because she mentioned his name and said he's working out in West Texas, but that's all I know about him."

Whitfield's voice was even sharper as he said, "I don't take kindly to being lied to, Mr. Kingfisher, especially by outsiders. I know good and well Larry Don Barlow skipped bail down

KINGFISHER *P.I.* ◆ 103

there where you come from and is a fugitive. I got the same alert that the Nueces County Sheriff's Department sent out to every law enforcement agency in the state. And the sheriff in Nueces County sent me a personal email, too, because he knew that Larry Don comes from this part of the country. It makes sense that you'd be looking for him, especially since Bucko Corcoran is the one who handled the bond for him. You've done work for Mr. Corcoran before."

Joseph looked at Whitfield with narrowed eyes for a long moment before saying, "You and the sheriff down there have been burning up the Internet with emails this afternoon, haven't you?"

"I try to stay on good terms with all my fellow law enforcement officers. I've found that it pays dividends in the long run."

Joseph looked at Callie. She returned the look levelly but didn't offer him any advice. This was his business, not hers. She had no idea how stubborn he ought to be about admitting the truth. It looked like Whitfield had a pretty good handle on the situation, though, and he didn't seem like the sort of man whose mind would be easy to change once he'd made it up.

"All right," Joseph said abruptly. "I'm working for Bucko, and I'm looking for Larry Don Barlow. And I'm within my legal rights to do both of those things."

"Nobody's arguing otherwise."

"The question now is . . . which side are you on, Sheriff?"

For a second, Callie thought that Joseph had stepped over a line that he shouldn't have. The pleasantly neutral and politely interested expression on Whitfield's face vanished. He sat up straighter in the comfortable armchair.

"I'm on the side of the law, nothing else," he said. "You'd do well not to forget that."

"Don't get me wrong, Sheriff, but I was under the impression that the Barlows have a lot of friends in this area, as well as their share of enemies. You can't blame me for wanting to know where on that spectrum you fall."

"The Barlows are one of the biggest crime families in East Texas. Where do *you* think I fall?"

Callie couldn't help but speak up. "I know this Larry Don is some sort of car thief, but the other two Barlows I've met don't seem so bad."

"Larry Don's more than a car thief."

"He was arrested for delivering a bunch of stolen cars to a chop shop down in Corpus," Joseph said. "Nobody said anything about him being part of some . . . criminal empire."

Whitfield nodded. "If your employer didn't mention that part, that's something you ought to take up with him."

"I intend to, once this job is over."

"As for Larry Don Barlow, it's true, he was arrested for delivering stolen cars and being an accessory to grand theft auto. But he's been in and out of trouble with the law dozens of times up here in Hackberry County and the surrounding area, and so have most of the other members of his family. Larry Don has a record going back to when he was fourteen years old. They got him then for delivering moonshine."

"Moonshine?" Callie repeated. "Is that still a thing?"

Whitfield leaned back and looked a bit less tense now that they were talking openly. "Absolutely," he told her.

"Moonshine is still big business in some parts of the country. Some people don't like paying taxes on liquor, and they think the homemade stuff has a better kick, too. But Larry Don and some of the other Barlows have also been arrested for grand theft, burglary, possession of a controlled substance with intent to distribute, accessory to prostitution, conspiracy, kidnapping, assault, and attempted murder."

He rattled off the charges as if he'd recently looked them up in some database . . . which he probably had, Callie thought.

Joseph asked, "Is there anything he *hasn't* done?"

"Plenty, I'm sure. He's never been charged him with cooking meth or actually killing anybody. The Texas Rangers suspect there are bodies buried in the Piney Woods that Larry Don is responsible for, but they've never been able to get the evidence they need to charge him. Mind you, I'm not convinced he's guilty of those killings. I don't believe he's a cold-blooded murderer." Whitfield shrugged. "But I could be wrong about that. It's been known to happen."

Not that often, Callie suspected. She would have bet that Whitfield's track record as a lawman was pretty good.

"I'll ask you straight out," Joseph said. "Do you think Barlow is hiding somewhere around here?"

Callie added, "Out there at Froggy's, you asked Julie about her dad. Were you trying to get information from her because he's a fugitive?"

Whitfield leveled his gaze at her. "I didn't realize you're a private investigator, too, Ms. Kingfisher."

"I'm not, but I'm giving Joseph a hand with this case." She

paused, then said, "You don't have to be a licensed PI to work as a bail recovery agent in Texas."

"That's right, you don't," the sheriff admitted. "Most of them are, though."

"Maybe that's what I'm planning to do."

"Instead of going back into stunt work? I read about that accident you had. Seems like a mighty dangerous line of work you're in." He nodded toward the cane she had leaned against the foot of the bed. "You don't look like you really need that."

"Just now and then," she said. "And my future plans don't really seem relevant."

"You're the one who brought 'em up," Whitfield said.

"To get back to Larry Don Barlow . . ." Joseph said.

Whitfield shook his head. "I don't know where he is. That's the truth. If you think I might be helping him hide out, you can forget about that. He's a wanted fugitive to me, that's all. If I come across him, I'll arrest him and ship him back down to Nueces County so fast it'll make your head spin."

"Fair enough." Joseph waited a second, then asked, "What about the Wolvertons?"

Whitfield drew in a sharp breath. He seemed genuinely surprised as he said, "What *about* the Wolvertons? How do you even know about them?"

"We heard talk," Joseph replied off-handedly. "Something about some sort of bad blood between them and the Barlows?"

Whitfield came to his feet. "You stay away from the Wolvertons, you hear me? If you think poking around that bunch might help you find Larry Don, you just forget it." He slapped his hat on, gave Joseph and Callie grim looks in turn, and added, "That's an order."

With that, he turned and went to the door, pulled it open, and strode out into the gathering dusk, leaving Callie and Joseph sitting there looking at each other in puzzlement.

Chapter 14

"Do you think maybe he's tied in with the Wolvertons somehow?" Callie asked a short time later. "Like, maybe one of those shirttail relatives Julie was talking about?"

"Possibly," Joseph said. "He certainly was adamant about us staying away from them."

Callie sighed and said, "I hope he's not part of that bunch. He seemed like an honest man who's just trying to do his job."

They were sitting in the coffee shop across the parking lot from the lodge's rooms, tucked away in a back corner booth with no one sitting near them. They kept their voices low so the conversation wouldn't be overheard.

"He struck me as honest, too," Joseph said, "but you never know." He glanced toward the counter. "Here comes our food."

A fortyish woman with dark hair, wearing a uniform with the name "Deborah" stitched onto it, expertly delivered two plates with burgers and fries on them.

"There you go, folks," she said. "Anything else I can get for y'all? Want me to top off those iced teas?"

"That would be fine," Joseph told her. "But we don't need anything other than that."

"Gotcha. I'll be back with a pitcher of tea."

"You know, even drinking this much caffeine, I think I'll be able to sleep tonight," Callie commented once Deborah was gone. She yawned to emphasize the point.

"You'll need to be alert for a while yet," Joseph told her. "The evening isn't over."

Callie frowned across the table at her brother. "After everything we've already done today, what else did you have in mind?"

"I thought I'd have a look at the Barlow place. Of course, you don't have to come along—"

"Hold on, hold on. I came to help you with this case. You're not going to get rid of me that easily."

"I'm not trying to get rid of you. I'm just saying that you don't have to feel like I'm expecting you to come along on everything I do."

"You know where to find Larry Don's house?"

"I have the address, and I've studied it by looking at it online, but there's something about actually laying eyes on a place . . . You just can't get the same sort of feel for a location on-line."

"Count me in," Callie said. She picked up her hamburger, which was thick and juicy and had two slices of cheese and four pieces of bacon on it. It wasn't the least bit healthy, and as someone who had always tried to stay physically fit—for both professional and personal reasons—she knew she shouldn't eat like this.

Sometimes, though, she just had to. Maybe she was part barbarian and had to have some red meat now and then. That was one reason she had gone into stunt work. She couldn't see starving herself to meet Hollywood standards. True, she had a little more heft to her than many of the actresses she doubled for, but costuming and camera angles were able to hide that almost completely.

The food was good, nothing special but tasty and filling. The iced tea was brewed strong. Callie felt just on the verge of being uncomfortably full as she and Joseph walked back across the parking lot toward their rooms.

"When are you going to take that little jaunt you mentioned?" Callie asked. She didn't see anybody around, but she didn't want to get too specific about what she was saying, despite that.

"In another hour or two," he replied. "I want it late enough that there won't be many people around."

"All right. That'll give us both a chance to rest a little." She paused, then added sternly, "Don't even think about sneaking off without me, you got it?"

Joseph chuckled and said, "Got it."

She wasn't sure whether to believe him or not. For the most part, Joseph was honest and trustworthy, she believed, but he might decide that lying to her was all right, as long as it was to protect her.

On the other hand, he had allowed her to come along on this case, so he must have intended to include her in his search for Larry Don Barlow.

At some point, the doors of the rooms at the Slumbering Pines Lodge had been upgraded to use card keys. Callie slipped hers out of her jeans pocket, inserted it into the slot above the door handle, and pulled it out when the light flashed green. She opened the door and stepped into the room. She heard Joseph's door close, one room over.

Her own door swung shut behind her, despite the fact that she twisted around swiftly and made a grab for it. Instinct prompted the reaction, but the alarm bells hadn't kicked in quite soon enough when Callie caught the smell of tobacco in the room.

She didn't smoke. Never had.

She missed the door. It closed with a solid thump.

The next instant, somebody rammed into her from behind. The impact would have made her stagger if an arm hadn't wrapped around her waist. She opened her mouth to yell, but a hand clamped over her mouth before she could get a sound out.

"I got her!" a man rasped in her ear. "I got the little bi—"

Still acting out of instinct, and muscle memory from basic training and the MMA ring and the hundreds of fight scenes she had done in movies, Callie brought up the cane and rammed the end of it behind her as hard as she could. The ferrule sank into something soft, and the man's triumphant exclamation ended abruptly as beer-laden breath exploded from his mouth in a gasp of pain. His hand fell away from her mouth, but he was able to keep hugging her awkwardly with his other arm. Both of them staggered from side to side.

Callie could have yelled for Joseph's help then, but she was mad and wanted to lash out on her own. She lifted the cane again, held it with both hands around the middle of its length, and struck behind her with the handle, aiming the blow over her right shoulder. It thudded solidly against something, either her attacker's head or his shoulder.

She hoped it was his head.

This time he let go of her. He groaned, and even though it was too dark in the room to be sure, she thought he fell to the floor.

He wasn't alone, she knew. He had been crowing to somebody about grabbing her.

Footsteps scuffed on the carpet in front of her. She dropped her grip to the end of the cane and swung it like a baseball bat at arm level through the darkened space in front of her.

Again she wasn't in time. She hit something, but the second man was already too close to her and still coming. His momentum carried him forward into her. He was big enough that his weight forced Callie backward. She stumbled over something—probably the guy she had knocked down a few seconds earlier—and fell, landing hard on her butt.

"Get her, Earl!"

That voice came from somewhere else in the room. So there were *three* of them, at least. Callie remembered that one of the Wolvertons in the big truck that had tried to crush them was named Earl, according to Froggy.

Somehow, the Wolvertons had tracked her down and wanted revenge because she and Joseph had interfered with their attack on Julie Barlow.

And maybe revenge for more than that, she thought,

remembering how one of the motorcycles chasing them had wrecked. Crashes like that could be fatal.

But she couldn't worry about that now. She was outnumbered, and the man she had tripped and fallen over was still conscious. A wildly flailing hand closed on her shoulder.

"Here she is!"

She twisted and rolled. Her mixed martial arts training came back to her again. She aimed a stiff-armed blow at the sound of the voice. The heel of her hand collided hard with a man's chin. She felt his head jerk back.

She had lost the cane when she fell. Levering herself up on her other arm, she dropped on top of the man she had just struck. As she landed, she sunk her knee into his midsection.

Maybe a little bit *south* of his midsection, because he screamed and jackknifed underneath her.

Up until now, the fight hadn't generated much noise, just a few thuds and grunts. But that shriek of agony ended any hopes the invaders might have had of grabbing her quietly. They probably knew that her brother was right next door, and since their ambush had gone awry, they might not want to hang around and wait for the odds against them to get worse.

Just to make sure of that, Callie yelled, *"Joey!"*

Somebody yanked the door open. Light from outside spilled into the room. Callie saw a figure dart through the opening, followed by running footsteps pounding on the asphalt parking lot. Another man followed, moving fast as he, too, tried to make his getaway.

That left the one on the floor. He was still moaning in pain as he rolled onto his hands and knees, but desperation kept him moving.

Callie said, "No, you don't!" and lunged at him as he tried to struggle to his feet. She wanted to have at least one of them here to turn over to Sheriff Whitfield.

He writhed like a snake and lashed out, swinging an arm that caught Callie full in the face. She fell back and rolled over onto her stomach. The man scrambled to his feet and headed for the door in a stumbling run.

The opening was blocked suddenly. "Hey!" Joseph said. "Hold it right there!"

The man didn't even slow down. He lowered a shoulder and barreled into Joseph like a fullback going for the goal line. Joseph must not have had time to get his feet set. He went over backward just as Callie had a few minutes earlier. The fleeing man hurdled over him and kept going.

Lying on her belly this way, Callie realized she still had the Smith & Wesson Shield in the holster under her shirt. She felt it pressing into her stomach. She thought about pulling the 9mm and firing a shot after the man, but she discarded the idea almost instantly. Throwing bullets blindly out into the night that way, especially with the coffee shop on the other side of the parking lot, would be the height of carelessness.

Besides, she didn't want to risk killing anybody unless there was absolutely no other alternative.

She pushed herself up and hurried to the doorway. Her leg ached, but she ignored it. Joseph was still lying there. She hoped he wasn't hurt too badly. As she heard him wheezing, she realized that the collision must have knocked all the air out of him, and he was trying to get his breath back.

She dropped to a knee beside him as somewhere else in the parking lot, an engine roared to life. A second later, tires squealed and gravel flew. Headlights flashed on. She didn't get a good look at the vehicle, but she thought it was a big SUV that rumbled out of the lot and screeched onto the highway.

"Joey, are you all right?" she asked. She got an arm around his shoulders and helped him sit up. His gasping seemed to ease a little. After a moment, he was able to take a couple of deep breaths, and then he nodded.

"I'm fine," he said. "What was that about?"

Before Callie could answer, a middle-aged man and woman, probably guests here at the lodge, approached them warily along the sidewalk in front of the rooms.

"Say, are you folks all right?" the man called.

"Yes, just a little trouble, but it's all over now," Callie said. "No one was hurt."

She hoped that wasn't strictly true. She hoped the guy who had caught her knee in his nether regions was still in great pain.

"What happened?" the woman wanted to know. They came a little closer now that it looked like there wasn't any danger.

"Someone had broken into my room," Callie said. "We chased them off."

"Oh, my!" the woman said.

"Should we call the police?" the man asked as he tried to get a phone out of his shirt pocket.

"No, there's no need for that."

Since they hadn't managed to catch any of the intruders,

she wanted to wait until she'd had a chance to talk to Joseph before they involved the authorities . . . *if* they involved the authorities.

She went on, "I'll take a look around in there and see if they managed to steal anything. If they did, then I'll call the cops."

"Well, if you're sure . . ." The man let his phone slide back into his pocket.

"What about an ambulance?" the woman asked.

"No, I'm fine," Joseph said. "One of them just bowled me over and knocked the wind out of me when he ran into me. How about you, Callie?"

"They startled me, that's all," she lied. The incident had been considerably more than that, but she wasn't injured and didn't need any medical attention.

The couple made sympathetic noises for a minute or so longer, then returned to their room, obviously glad that it hadn't been them on the receiving end of a would-be burglary.

Callie helped Joseph to his feet, and as he brushed himself off, he asked quietly, "Those weren't just sneak thieves, were they?"

"One of them mentioned the name Earl," she replied. "That's the name of one of the Wolvertons."

"Sheriff Whitfield warned us not to go looking for them," Joseph mused with a shake of his head. "But he didn't say anything about *them* looking for *us.*"

CHAPTER 15

Considering the fact that both of them were shaken up, even though they actually hadn't been injured, they decided that the expedition to check out the Barlow house could wait.

"It's been too long a day," Joseph said. "We should get some rest, so we can look at everything with clearer eyes in the morning."

"Breakfast in the coffee shop?"

"Sounds good. Eight o'clock?"

"I'll be there," Callie said, even though that seemed pretty early to her. She supposed Joseph wanted to get a good running start on the day, and she couldn't blame him for that.

Back in her room, she looked around to make sure the Wolvertons hadn't stolen or bothered anything. Nothing appeared to be out of place. They had just wanted *her*.

She also examined the door and saw no signs of tampering with the lock or the door itself. It hadn't been forced open.

That meant they'd used a key to get in here. She considered the possibility that Dennis Ordway had helped them. He was supposed to be related to the Barlows by marriage. It seemed unlikely that he would have cooperated with the Wolvertons.

But you never could be sure about things like that. Maybe not everybody had a price . . . but most people sure as blazes did.

There were other explanations, though, Callie told herself, other ways the Wolvertons could have gotten their hands on a passkey. Housekeeping had to be able to get into all the rooms. That was an angle she and Joseph could look into later, if they needed to.

For now, she wedged a chair under the door handle and went into the bathroom to take a hot shower, hoping it would ease some of her aches. After she dried off, including blow drying her hair until it was semi-dry, she put on the oversized t-shirt in which she slept, swallowed a couple of aspirin, and climbed into bed.

No nightmares—about Vickie's disappearance or anything else—haunted her sleep that night. She was up early, showered and dressed, and she moved the curtain back a little so she could check outside the window before she unfastened both locks on the door and moved the chair she had propped under the door handle.

She didn't see any signs of potential trouble. In fact, it looked like Joseph had just left his room, because he was strolling across the parking lot toward the coffee shop. Quickly, Callie moved the chair, unlocked the door, and stepped outside. She patted the pocket of her jeans, just to make sure the card key was there, and pulled the door closed behind her as she called, "Hey, wait up."

He stopped and turned toward her as she walked after him, using the cane but not actually putting much weight on it.

"How are you this morning?" he asked. "Sleep all right?"

"Yeah, better than I expected, really," she said. "How about you?"

"A few bumps and bruises," he replied with a shrug. "Nothing important."

"Same for me." She glanced up at the blue sky, dotted with fluffy white clouds above the towering pines, and added, "Looks like it's going to be a nice day."

"Callie Kingfisher!"

The unexpected hail came from a woman who had just stepped out of the coffee shop as they approached. She walked quickly toward them, her high heels clicking on the asphalt. She wore tight white jeans and a deep blue, long-sleeved silk shirt. Elaborate bracelets hung from her wrists. Long, light brown hair tumbled around her shoulders and down her back. Sunglasses even darker than those favored by Sheriff Howard Whitfield covered her eyes.

A young man emerged from the diner and hurried after her. He was heavyset, with a shock of curly dark hair and black-framed glasses. Another man followed him, this one tall and solidly built, mostly bald, with an open, amiable face and a decidedly casual air about him.

"Who's that?" Joseph asked under his breath.

Even though the woman coming toward them looked familiar, Callie couldn't place her at first. Then a memory clicked into place, and she said, equally quietly, "Somebody I never expected to see in Hackberry, Texas."

A friendly smile was on the woman's lips as she came up to them, but the dark glasses prevented Callie from seeing if the expression was reflected in the woman's eyes.

"I saw you through the window there, and for a second I just couldn't believe it was you," the woman said. "But let's admit it, it's pretty hard to mistake you for anyone else, Callie. It's so good to see you again! I heard about that terrible accident, but you look like you're doing all right now. How *are* you, dear?"

"I'm fine, Felicity," Callie said.

The woman called Felicity looked Joseph up and down and asked, "And who's this?"

"My brother, Joseph Kingfisher." Callie didn't see any way of avoiding introductions, so she went on, "Joseph, this is Felicity Prosper. She's a, ah, journalist."

Felicity's lips tightened for a second at the hesitation in Callie's voice, but then she smiled and extended her hand to Joseph.

"It's so nice to meet you," she said. "And now I can see the resemblance."

Joseph shook hands with her. As usual, he was a little reserved in the presence of an attractive woman and said, "It's a pleasure to meet you, Ms. Prosper. If you don't mind me asking, how do you know my sister?"

"Oh, I did a story about her for *Inside Beat* a couple of years ago," Felicity replied with a casual wave. "That's the show I work for. We did a series on the leading stunt performers in Hollywood."

"I see," Joseph said, nodding. "Now that you mention it, I

do remember hearing about that. I'm afraid I didn't see it, though."

"I sent you a DVD," Callie said.

"I know, and I should have gotten around to it—"

"You can stream that episode now, too," Felicity said. "In fact, you can stream everything on *Inside Beat* going back five seasons."

"I'll have to keep that in mind," Joseph said. "Now, if you'll excuse us—"

"Wait a minute," the young man with Felicity interrupted. "Joseph Kingfisher. You're the private detective."

Callie and Joseph were both surprised. "How do you know that?" Callie asked.

Felicity said, "Oh, Josh is a wizard at research. He can find out anything about anybody . . . which comes in handy sometimes." She moved a step closer to Joseph. "You're a private detective? How fascinating!"

The young man called Josh pushed up the glasses that had slid down his nose and said, "I'm Josh Green, Mr. Kingfisher. I produce Felicity's segments on *Inside Beat*. When we did the feature on your sister, I compiled a lot of background information on your family, just in case we needed to use any of it on the show." He paused and frowned. "In fact, don't I recall there was something about another sister . . .?"

"She passed away," Joseph said, his voice flinty and unfriendly now.

Josh Green's eyes widened behind the glasses. "Oh, my, I'm so sorry! I didn't mean to bring up painful memories—"

Joseph cut him off with a curt head-shake. "That's all right.

It was a long time ago."

Felicity bulled right through that momentary awkwardness by saying, "What in the world brings a Hollywood stuntwoman and a private eye to a place like this?"

She waved both hands this time to take in their surroundings.

"I could ask the same of a tabloid TV personality," Callie responded bluntly.

"*Inside Beat* is a news and investigative journalism series," Felicity said. "It's not a tabloid."

Callie just shrugged, as if to say that she didn't see any difference. Which she didn't. Shows like *Inside Beat* were just a fact of life in Hollywood; dozens of them could be found on cable and in syndication and now on streaming services or as podcasts. They pretended to be hard-hitting journalism, but in reality they were just publicity tools, focused on glitz and glamour and easily manipulated into covering whatever was trendy. Callie thought that Felicity and *Inside Beat* had actually done all right by her and hadn't made her look like some sort of freak, but that didn't raise her overall opinion of this type of series.

"In fact, Josh and Nick and I have come here to cover a news story," Felicity went on.

The tall, balding man took that as his cue to extend a hand to Joseph. "Hiya," he said. "I'm Nick Baker. Cameraman and driver."

Joseph shook with him and said, "Hello, Nick."

"Are you really a private eye?"

"A private investigator, yes."

"Joe Kingfisher, Private Eye," Nick said in the deep tones of an announcer. "A Quinn Martin Production." Then, "Sorry, you're all too young for that reference."

"No, I'm not," Felicity snapped, then said, "No, wait . . . Never mind! Why don't we all go back in this charming establishment and we can talk more while we have breakfast? The boys and I had just sat down and hadn't ordered yet when I spotted you out here in the parking lot, Callie, and was so surprised to see you that I simply had to come out and say hello."

"Yes, come join us," Josh invited. "We'll put it on the expense account."

Felicity shot him a narrow-eyed glance, as if he hadn't had to go *that* far to be friendly, but she was still smiling as she said, "Please."

Joseph, clearly out of his depth, looked to Callie for a decision. She didn't particularly want to sit down and have breakfast with Felicity Prosper . . . but she still planned to go back to Hollywood and return to stunt work sometime in the future, and it never hurt to have friends in the media . . .

She smiled and said, "Sure, we'd be happy to join you."

The waitress named Deborah was working again this morning, even though she had pulled the evening shift the night before. She looked tired but managed to smile when the group came in.

"The way you folks hurried out of here, I thought I'd done something wrong," she said to Felicity, Josh, and Nick.

"No, we just saw someone we know outside and wanted to ask them to join us," Felicity said. "We'll need a bigger table . . ."

"Sure, right back here."

She led them to a table and left them with menus, promising to return with coffee all around if that was what everyone wanted. Nods confirmed that.

Callie was at one end of the table, Felicity at the other. Joseph sat to Callie's right, with Nick next to him. Josh was across the table from Nick, with an empty chair between him and Callie. Felicity had taken off the dark glasses once they were inside. She looked at Callie over the menu in her hands and said, "You never did tell us what the two of you are doing here in . . ." She glanced at Josh. "What's the name of this town, again?"

"Hackberry," he supplied. "Like the tree."

"There's a tree with that name?"

"Yes, and that's what the county is called, too."

"Okay. But these are pine trees all around, right?"

"Yes. Mostly."

"Then why do they call it Hackberry?" Felicity shook her head. "You know what, never mind. That's not important." She smiled at Callie and Joseph. "Not as important as whatever brings you two here. Unless you're . . . sightseeing?"

"Family business," Joseph said. "We're looking for the right rest home for our grandfather."

Callie was glad he had decided to use that cover story. If Felicity Prosper knew they were actually working as bounty hunters at the moment, Callie had no doubt she would try to horn in on the case, thinking that it would be a good story.

"How sweet." Felicity was already losing interest. That was a good thing.

"We're here tracking down a crime story," Josh said

eagerly. "The show's sent us to Texas a couple of times before to cover big, important murder cases."

"Really?" Joseph said.

"Yeah. Well . . . one of them didn't start out to be a murder case. It was more like . . . a chili cook-off. But somebody got killed, and we were there to get the scoop."

"They still use the word *scoop* in the news business?" Callie asked.

"Sure, sometimes. So now we, uh, cover the crime beat for *Inside Beat*, I guess you could say."

Callie couldn't help but like the guy. He reminded her of a big, friendly puppy. Even though she knew better because of the job that had brought them here and the things they had discovered already, she said, "Hackberry doesn't exactly strike me as a hotbed of crime."

"Oh, but it is." Josh leaned forward and lowered his voice to a conspiratorial tone, but it was still loud enough to be heard easily. "One of the worst white supremacist organizations in the country operates around here. Most of them are members of the same family, actually, called the Barlows."

Deborah was approaching the table carrying a tray with an insulated carafe of coffee and five cups on it. The whole thing slipped out of her hands and came crashing down on the floor.

Chapter 16

Felicity leaped to her feet and backed away quickly, as if afraid that some of the spilled coffee was going to get on her expensive shoes or her white jeans, even though none of it actually came close to her.

Looking flustered and upset, Deborah knelt and started trying to clean up the mess, saying, "I'm sorry, I don't know what happened, I'm not usually so clumsy, I never drop any-thing—"

Nick got up from his chair and went to a knee. He said, "Here, let me give you a hand," as he began gathering up pieces of broken cups.

"Thank you," Deborah said. She picked up the carafe before more coffee could leak from it. Luckily, its spout had remained mostly closed, so not much had spilled. A busboy hurried over with some rags to mop up what had run out of the container while Nick and Deborah picked up the shattered remnants of the cups.

Deborah continued apologizing until Nick grinned and

said, "Hey, 's okay, it was an accident. You should see some of the messes *I've* made."

"That's nice of you to say, sir, but—"

"Nick. Nick Baker."

"I appreciate that, Mr. Baker, but I *never* drop things like that."

And why had she? Callie wondered as she sat at the table with the others. Was it just coincidence that Deborah had been rattled enough to drop that tray just as Josh mentioned the Barlows?

And what was that about them being white supremacists? Callie hadn't heard anything like that so far, and Sheriff Whitfield hadn't mentioned it when he was talking about the Barlow family the day before.

Now that Felicity's outfit was no longer in any imminent danger, she sat down again and said to Josh, "I shouldn't have to remind you of this since you're the producer, but it's probably not a good idea to talk about stories we're currently investigating."

The young man looked embarrassed but stood his ground. "I thought maybe Mr. Kingfisher would like to comment. As a private detective, he's not actually a member of law enforcement, but he probably knows a lot about crime and criminal organizations." He looked at Joseph. "How about it, Mr. Kingfisher? What can you tell me about white supremacist groups in this area?"

"Not a thing," Joseph replied, the words both blunt and emphatic. "Actually, this is the first I've heard of it. Callie and I are here on family business, not work-related." He paused, then added, "I will say, though, that the number of actual white supremacists in this country strikes me as being dramatically overinflated by the media."

"Oh?" Felicity said, her voice cool now. "And why would we do that?"

"I don't know. Because buzzwords and outrage make for good stories? More clicks and views?"

The two of them were starting to glare daggers at each other. Callie found herself in the unusual position of trying to be a peacemaker when she said, "Why don't we just have a good breakfast and not get started arguing politics? That never goes well."

"No, I suppose it doesn't," Felicity admitted.

Nick straightened from where he'd been kneeling on the floor. The mess from the dropped tray was cleaned up now, so he took his seat again.

Deborah said, "I'll go get a fresh pot of coffee. And I *won't* drop it this time, I promise."

She was true to her word and there were no more mishaps during breakfast. The pancakes, bacon, and scrambled eggs Callie ate weren't any healthier than the burger she'd had the night before, but they were equally decadent and good. She needed to be careful on this trip to Texas, she warned herself, or else she'd need to go on a strict diet by the time she got back to California.

If she got back to California. She wasn't sure where that thought came from, but it definitely crossed her mind for a moment.

"How long are you going to be in town?" Josh asked Callie

as they were finishing up the meal.

"I don't know for sure. Today and tonight, certainly, and after that we'll just have to see how it goes."

"With the retirement home, you mean."

"Right." Callie indulged her curiosity and asked, "How long will the three of you be here?"

Felicity answered instead of Josh. "As long as it takes to get the story. We don't leave without it, right, boys?"

Josh said, "That's right," and Nick just grunted something that could have been agreement as he wiped up the last of some over-easy egg yolks with a piece of biscuit.

When Deborah brought the check, Josh took it. "Corporate credit card," he said as he reached for his wallet.

"Pay up at the register, hon," Deborah told him.

"Oh. Sure."

Joseph said, "You really don't have to pay for our meal—"

"No, it's on us," Felicity interrupted him. "Josh can mark it down as research. We did ask you for your professional opinion, after all."

"About the white supremacists?"

"That's right. And it counts whether you believe in them or not."

"I never said I didn't believe in them. Just that their numbers aren't as impressive as the media would like to make them out to be."

Felicity shrugged. "Whatever."

As they all stood up and headed toward the entrance, Callie saw Nick lean in toward Josh's ear and heard him say quietly, "Give that poor gal a good tip."

"Really? The one who dropped that tray?"

"It wasn't her fault. She was shook up about something."

Josh shrugged. "Sure. It all goes on the expense account, anyway."

Callie hesitated and put a hand on Joseph's arm. "I'll catch up to you in a minute," she told him.

"Something wrong?" he asked with a slight frown.

"No, nothing. Just give me a minute and I'll see you over at our rooms."

"Fine," he said, and followed Felicity and Nick outside while Josh paused at the register to pay the check.

Callie turned around and spotted Deborah standing at the far end of the counter. She headed toward the waitress.

Deborah was writing something down in the ticket book she used to take orders. She glanced up as Callie approached, closed the book, and asked, "Did you forget something, ma'am?"

"No, I just wanted to talk to you for a second."

"I sure am sorry about what happened earlier—"

Callie shook her head and waved that off. "No need. I worked as a server for a little while, a long time ago. It's a hard job. But I wanted to ask you . . . Do you happen to be related to the Barlows?"

Deborah's eyes widened slightly. "The Barlows? What do you know about them?"

"Not much, but I met a couple of them yesterday and they seemed like pretty nice folks. They sure didn't strike me as being the sort who'd be mixed up in something as ugly as, well, being white supremacists."

Deborah's expression hardened as she said, "They're not. And to answer your question, no, I'm not related to the Barlows, but I grew up with three or four of them and have known the family pretty much my whole life. I don't like folks spreading lies about them . . . especially *Hollywood* people."

Callie didn't mention that she was one of those Hollywood people, sort of. The longer she was back in Texas, the easier it was to slip back into the mindset of being a Texan, she had discovered.

"If it's not true, why does that news producer think it is?"

"Because he's willing to believe anything bad he hears about folks he considers to be backwoods, redneck racists, I suppose." Deborah took a deep breath to control the anger she obviously felt. "I'm sorry, I shouldn't start spouting off. It's true, there have been plenty of folks in this part of the country who held some pretty backwards beliefs. Still are, I'm sure. And there was a time when the Klan was big around here. But that was a hundred years ago. In this job, I see a lot of folks of all colors, and nearly all of them just want to be left alone to live their lives. They're not out to cause trouble for anybody."

"Well, that's good to hear," Callie said. "But it doesn't explain why the Barlows have been tagged with that accusation."

Deborah looked around. No one was standing near them. She hesitated a second longer, then said, "Mount Ebenezer."

"What's that?"

"Methodist Church up in the northeast part of the county. There's a little community there, also called Mount Ebenezer. Most of the folks who live there are black."

"Something happened to the church?" Callie guessed.

"A month or so ago, it burned. Not to the ground, but it was damaged real bad. County fire marshal said it was arson. The sheriff found evidence linking it to the Barlows, or at least that's the rumor."

"What sort of evidence?"

"I don't have any idea," Deborah replied. "Like I said, it was just rumors that went around. But a while back, somebody vandalized an old black cemetery in another part of the county, and folks whispered that the Barlows had something to do with that, too. And there have been other things . . . black folks shot at, run off the road . . . I heard that warnings were delivered to some of the preachers saying that any black folks caught out after sundown would be shot . . . or strung up. Only those warnings didn't call them black folks, if you know what I mean."

"But you don't believe the Barlows had anything to do with all that?" Callie prompted.

"The ones I know wouldn't have acted like that." Deborah shrugged. "But shoot, I don't know the whole family. They're too spread out for that. You'll almost find a Barlow behind every other tree in the county."

"I heard that there's another family like that. The Wolvertons?"

Deborah's mouth twisted, as if she had bitten into something sour.

"I went to school with some of the Wolvertons, too. A really sorry, no-count bunch, if you ask me."

"Maybe they're the ones behind all the trouble," Callie

suggested.

"Oh, they're troublemakers, all right, but I've never heard anything bad about 'em where racial stuff is concerned. Fact of the matter is, there's been several black people married into the family. They're not prejudiced." Deborah snorted in contempt. "Just mean, nasty jackasses."

"Well, I don't want to have anything to do with *them.*"

"No, ma'am, you do not." Deborah picked up her ticket book, as if she had to get back to work, but before she did, she cocked her head to the side a little and said, "If you don't mind my askin', why are you so interested in all this stuff?"

"I just wanted to find out what sort of place Hackberry County is," Callie said. "I don't know if you heard us talking about it or not, but my brother and I are thinking about moving our grandfather into the retirement home here."

"Sleepy Pines? Oh, it's a fine place. My friend Donna runs it, and she makes sure things are done right."

"Maybe so, but it sounds like there are a lot of things going on around here that are a little shady . . ."

"Now, don't y'all get scared off by what I said! Goodness' sake, most of the folks in the county are fine, upstanding, law-abiding people just like you'd find anywhere else. There are *always* gonna be a few troublemakers around, anywhere you go."

"That's true." Callie nodded. "I'll think about what you said. I appreciate you being so candid with me."

"I'm in the habit of telling the truth."

"That's the best way to be," Callie agreed. She smiled and left the coffee shop. The trio from *Inside Beat* were nowhere in sight, and she didn't see Joseph, either. She walked across the parking lot and knocked on the door of his room.

"I was beginning to wonder if you'd gotten lost," he said when he opened it a moment later.

"No, but I found out a few more things," Callie said. "And I think you'll want to hear about them."

CHAPTER 17

"Well, that sort of explains what that young man was talking about," Joseph said a short time later after Callie had summarized her conversation with Deborah. They were in Joseph's room. "It sounds as if this whole business about the Barlows being involved in hate crimes and white supremacy is a fairly recent development."

"What about the idea that the Wolvertons are really behind it?" Callie asked. "If they and the Barlows are rival gangs, I'd think that framing them for something like that would be a good strategy."

"It seems plausible," Joseph admitted. "But you said that waitress told you it wasn't possible."

"Yeah, but only because some of the Wolvertons are married to black people. They might go along with it if they believed it would put more money in the family's pockets in the long run . . . including *their* pockets."

"Or maybe the members of the family doing it simply haven't revealed their activities to everyone else. That's a possibility, too."

"Either way, the Barlows are the victims of being framed," Callie said.

"Or they actually *are* terrible enough to do such things," Joseph said. "Just because Julie seemed nice enough and her grandfather is a charming old man, it doesn't mean they're incapable of being bad people. 'A man may smile, and smile, and be a villain.'"

"I can quote Shakespeare, too, blast it. All I'm saying is that I'm going to reserve judgment on the Barlows."

"You heard all the charges against them that Sheriff Whitfield told us about. Like it or not, they *are* criminals."

"I never said they weren't," Callie muttered. "What now?"

"Let's go take a look at their house."

"You're sure you can find it?"

"I'm confident that I can."

"Confidence is a big part of any endeavor," Callie said.

"Who are you quoting?"

She smiled. "Me, as far as I know."

They left the motel room. As they stepped out onto the sidewalk, movement to her right caught Callie's eye. She looked along the walk and saw a housekeeper in a light blue uniform opening the door of one of the other rooms. The young Hispanic woman had a card key with a clip attached to it. She hung the clip back on her belt and pushed her cleaning supplies cart into the room. The door swung closed behind her.

"Did you see that?" Callie asked once they were in the pickup.

"See what?"

"That passkey the housekeeper used to get in probably hangs up somewhere when it's not being used. In a supply closet, maybe. If the Wolvertons knew that and snagged it somehow, that could be how they got into my room last night."

"That would be pretty careless," Joseph said. "More than likely, the passkey is kept in the office."

"Maybe. But they could have gotten their hands on it there, too. We don't know how diligent good old Dennis is about keeping an eye on things."

"No. We also don't know that he didn't just give it to the Wolvertons."

"And double-crossed his wife's family."

Joseph shrugged as he pushed the button on the dash to start the Ram's engine. "I suppose we could ask the Wolvertons, if we run into them again."

Callie shuddered and said, "Ugh. I'd rather not, thank you."

"It's possible they may not give us a choice. One more reason to keep our eyes open."

That sounded like good advice to Callie. She followed it, looking all around them as Joseph backed up and drove out of the lodge's parking lot.

She didn't see anything that looked the least bit suspicious, though.

Joseph put his phone in the holder on the dash designed for that purpose. He had a GPS app open.

"I know the truck has GPS, but I'm used to using my own,"

he explained.

"Hey, it doesn't matter to me," Callie said. "Whatever gets us to the right place."

As he followed the highway farther east out of Hackberry, he said, "It sounded like you did a good job talking to that waitress. There's a knack to interrogating someone without them knowing that they're being interrogated."

Callie shrugged and said, "I just talked to her."

"Well, you got some good information out of her. When we get back to the lodge, we can look up those incidents she mentioned and find out more about them. I'm curious as to whether or not the Barlows actually were involved in them . . . but at the same time, hate crimes don't really fall into the scope of our job."

"I know. We're just here to find Larry Don Barlow and take him back to Corpus Christi."

"Exactly." Joseph paused, then added, "It never hurts to know as much as possible about a fugitive's background, though. That might give you a clue where to look for him, or tell you what sort of reception you might get from those around him."

"Not a very cooperative reception, I imagine. From everything I've heard—and seen when those motorcycles were chasing us—it seems like the Barlows are surrounded by enemies."

"Perhaps well deserved enemies."

"Maybe," Callie said. She was still going to reserve judgment on that. "But either way, that's enough to make you paranoid and suspicious of stranger."

Joseph inclined his head in acknowledgment of that point.

As they left the town behind, the forest closed in again on both sides of the highway. There were occasional houses or roadside businesses where the thick growth had been cleared, but for the most part a seemingly unbroken line of pines bordered both sides of the road.

Here and there, dirt tracks just wide enough for a single vehicle branched off into the trees and quickly vanished. The presence of mailboxes at the head of those tracks told Callie there were houses back up there in the woods, completely invisible from the road.

If you were deep enough in there, Callie thought, it would feel like you were completely isolated from the world, like there was no one else around for miles, unable to see or hear any other signs of civilization. It actually gave her kind of a creepy feeling to ponder that, having spent years in the hustle and bustle and crowds of Southern California. She could barely imagine being cut off from the world like that.

As they came up on one of the little dirt roads that turned off into the woods, Joseph said, "According to the GPS, that should be it."

"We've come three or four miles from town," Callie said. "Julie acted like her home was close by and she could walk there from the lodge without any trouble."

"Maybe she went somewhere else. It's possible she doesn't live out here with her parents anymore. She's old enough to be living on her own."

"Yeah, I suppose that's true. Or maybe she called somebody else to come and get her."

"If we see her again, we could ask her, but it's not really any of our business. We need to concentrate on finding Larry Don."

He drove past the turn-off, prompting Callie to ask, "Where are you going?"

"We can't just drive in there for no good reason. In a place like this, they'd set the dogs on us, at the very least, and maybe even start shooting. I want to get closer and take a look without the Barlows knowing I'm around. According to the map, there's a county road up here about a quarter of a mile . . ."

The map was right. A paved road went both right and left from the highway. A sign on a post at the corner read CR258. Callie assumed the CR stood for "County Road". She couldn't explain the number. There certainly couldn't be 258 roads in Hackberry County. It wasn't that big.

Joseph turned left. The county road was fairly narrow and unmarked, but it was wide enough for two vehicles to pass each other, unlike the one-lane driveways they had seen up until now. He said, "I studied the area in satellite view on the map. The house and the other buildings are about half a mile in from the highway. I saw what looked like an abandoned building somewhere along here . . ."

"There it is," Callie said, pointing.

Joseph slowed. The square brick building on the left appeared to be deserted, all right. Most of the front wall was taken up by a roll-up door with some painted-over windows in it. To the left was a door marked *OFFICE*. Across the top of the building above the roll-up door were faded letters spelling out *HENDERSON GARAGE*. Weeds grew tall in front of the place. To the right of the building was a gravel parking area. More weeds sprouted here and there in the lot, but they hadn't taken it over yet. From the looks of it, the garage had been out of business for several years, at the very least.

Joseph turned and pulled through the gravel lot to the back of the building. It was overgrown with weeds back there, too, but the trees had been cleared away in an area large enough for several vehicles. Joseph parked behind the building where the pickup would be out of sight from the county road.

He killed the engine and said, "All right, you can wait here while I go through the woods and try to get close enough to the Barlow place to get a good look at it."

"Say what now?"

"You wait here—"

"No, no, I heard you the first time," Callie interrupted. "I just wondered who you thought you were talking to."

Joseph sighed. "Look, this is just a scouting mission, but it could be dangerous."

"More dangerous than what happened yesterday when the Wolvertons attacked us not once but *twice?* More dangerous than that?"

"Getting around in these woods isn't easy. You've got that bad leg—"

"It's fine," Callie lied. Actually, after all the strenuous activity yesterday, her leg ached quite a bit this morning, but she wasn't going to let Joseph use that as an excuse to leave her behind. "You asked for my help on this case. I know you probably just meant it as a distraction, but you're not going to push me aside now. After everything that's happened, I'm invested in finding Larry Don, too."

"I'd be wasting my time by arguing with you, wouldn't I?"

She had to smile at that. "You always have been."

After a moment, Joseph nodded. "All right. But I want you to promise me that if you find the going too hard, you'll come back here to the pickup and wait for me."

"Sure, I promise," Callie said, knowing full well that she had no intention of keeping that pledge.

"You *do* have that pistol I loaned you, don't you?"

"Yeah. Do you think we'll need guns?"

"Well, I certainly hope not. But I think it's better for us to be armed, just in case we have to deal with any . . . unforeseen problems."

They got out of the pickup and carefully closed the doors, pushing them up until they fastened instead of slamming them. Callie thought it was unlikely anybody was lurking nearby in the woods, but you never knew about such things.

Joseph led the way into the thick growth of trees. He had always had a better sense of direction than Callie, so she trusted him to know where he was going. He looked back over his shoulder at her and said quietly, "Watch where you put your feet. There are a lot of rattlesnakes in these woods."

"Now you tell me," she muttered.

"More than likely, they'll hear us coming and try to get out of our way. But they can be stubborn and aggressive at times, so just be careful."

"More than likely," Callie repeated under her breath as she warily eyed the ground, which was carpeted with fallen pine needles and the occasional clump of dead leaves from the underbrush.

The sun had been up long enough that the air was starting to get hot. It was still here in the trees, too, with not a breath of wind moving. Callie felt herself sweating before they had gone very far. The band holding the belly holster in place rubbed against her skin. It wasn't really uncomfortable, just annoying.

As were the mosquitoes that buzzed and whined around her head. She should have drenched herself in insect repellent, she thought as she waved her hand in front of her face in a largely futile attempt to discourage the hovering cloud of insects, but she hadn't realized that they were going to be traipsing around in the woods.

To be fair, she hadn't asked Joseph what they were going to be doing, either, so it wasn't really his fault.

As he'd suggested, she took a good look at the ground ahead of her every time she took a step. Once she thought she heard something rustling a short distance to her right and froze for a second, but she didn't see anything and moved on. She felt her heart beating faster. She didn't like snakes. Didn't like anything about them.

The going was difficult, as he had warned. The trees grew so close together that they had to hunt for gaps large enough to get through. They had to duck under numerous low-hanging branches. There wasn't a lot of undergrowth, but the plants that flourished in the perpetual shadow underneath the pines all seemed to have thorns on them. At times, Callie would have almost sworn that the briars reached out to snag her clothing and claw at her skin. She was already bleeding in several places, not enough to worry about but definitely irritating.

Somewhere up ahead, car doors slammed. A voice called out. Callie couldn't make out the words. Engine noise rose and then diminished.

Joseph held up a hand in a signal for her to stop, then looked back over his shoulder at her and whispered, "We're getting close now."

That was fine with Callie. She'd had enough of this jungle.

CHAPTER 18

Joseph knelt next to a tree and motioned Callie forward. She came up on the tree's other side and joined him, scanning the ground carefully for any sign of snakes before she put her knee down.

The pines still formed a screen in front of them, so the view wasn't a very good one, but through the gaps Callie was able to see several buildings and gradually formed a picture of the Barlow home place.

The main house was a huge, rambling, wooden two-story structure painted a light gray with white trim. It looked like it had been built at least a hundred years earlier. A covered porch ran around at least two sides and probably all the way around. Thick stone columns supported it. A balcony with its own wooden columns and roof overhung the porch on the front of the house. Above the balcony were two high-peaked dormer windows. The place had an ancient, gothic air about it.

The satellite dish mounted on the roof took away a little

from that effect.

So did the large metal building in the back. Two sets of wide double doors were open, revealing a concrete floor on which were parked a couple of jacked-up pickups with huge wheels, a dark blue Jeep Wrangler Rubicon, and a bright orange Kubota tractor with a front end loader on it. In addition, there were two empty spots where other vehicles could be parked. The one they had heard leaving had been in there, Callie speculated.

Also behind the house, but closer than the metal garage, was another old-looking building, this one made of what appeared to be irregular-shaped chunks of red and tan sandstone. It was a blockhouse topped by a circular wooden water tank. This far out of town and isolated as it was, the property probably had its own water well, and the well-head and storage tank, or tanks, would be inside that building. The tank on the roof would be a cistern to catch rainwater.

Two smaller metal storage buildings sat to the side. Their doors were closed, so Callie had no idea what might be inside them.

All the way on the other side of the house, underneath a tall carport that appeared to have been built specially for it, was a long, black-and-silver RV.

The trees had been cleared and the stumps uprooted in a large enough area for a well-kept lawn, complete with flower beds and some shrubbery, on all four sides of the house. That relieved the grim aspect of the place somewhat. Beyond the lawn, however, the trees were as thick as ever, looking impenetrable at first glance even though they actually weren't. The presence of Callie and Joseph proved that.

She leaned over to him and whispered, "Maybe we should get closer."

She started to stand up from where she was kneeling, but his hand on her shoulder stopped her.

"Wait," he breathed. Using the same hand, he pointed at the ground in front of them.

Callie had to study it for several moments before she saw what had alerted Joseph. A thin, almost invisible wire ran about six inches above the surface. Callie's eyes tried to follow it but lost sight of the wire in both directions. That was how small and cunningly concealed it was.

"Booby trap?" she whispered.

"An alarm, more likely," he replied. "I don't think they'd want to call more attention to themselves by rigging anything that would kill somebody. But either way, we don't want to trip it."

Callie agreed with that.

"We could step over that wire, if we were careful," she said.

"They probably have other security measures in place. Let's just watch for a while. Maybe we'll see something interesting."

Callie supposed that was possible. Someone had left not long before; they had heard the vehicle. Whoever it was could come back, or somebody else could leave.

She supposed it was too much to hope that Larry Don Barlow would step out into plain sight. She had studied the copies of the booking photos that Bucko Corcoran had given to Joseph. She believed she would recognize Larry Don if she saw him.

If they did lay eyes on him, what would they do then? Would their testimony be enough to convince Sheriff Whitfield to come out here and arrest him? Or would someone tip Larry Don off about any such attempt, causing him to flee again?

It would be better, Callie decided, if they were able to get Larry Don somewhere by himself and take him into custody. Of course, he might put up a fight, which meant she and Joseph would be legally justified in using force to apprehend him. At least, she assumed that was the case. Joseph knew the law; she would follow his lead . . . as long as he didn't hesitate too much.

Those thoughts ran through her mind as she knelt there and watched the Barlow place along with her brother. Time passed slowly, especially in this insect-laden, stifling heat. More than once she was about to slap at a mosquito when she caught herself and managed not to do it. She didn't want to make that much noise. Even though there were little sounds all around them in the forest, it would be better not to add anything unnatural to them.

She was tempted to sit down, too, but she felt so groggy, she knew if she did that she might go to sleep. And she didn't want to miss anything. So she wiped sweat and mosquitoes away from her face and tried to stay alert.

It helped when a screen door at the house opened and closed with a loud bang.

Callie leaned forward and peered through the gaps between the trees. She caught a glimpse of someone walking toward one of the smaller metal buildings behind the house. It was Julie Barlow, she realized. The blond hair was pulled into a ponytail today, and Julie wore cutoff jean shorts and a sleeveless t-shirt.

If she was going to be outside for very long, dressed like that, she'd better have used plenty of insect repellent, Callie thought.

Julie opened the storage building's door to reveal a zero-turn lawn mower with a big deck parked inside it. Looked like she was about to do some yard work. Callie leaned closer to Joseph and said, "When she fires up that mower, it'll make enough racket we could get closer without being heard."

He nodded. "It might be worth running the risk—" He stopped short, his head jerked around, and then his hand closed around Callie's arm. "Over there!" he breathed urgently. "Get behind that clump of brush!"

That clump of briars, that was what he meant, she thought as he urged her toward the thicker undergrowth. The stuff clawed at her clothes and penetrated to jab at her flesh as they skirted the edge of it. Then Joseph put a hand on her back to indicate that she was to get down. She grimaced as she stretched out on her belly, both from the thorns poking at her and the worry that a snake might be lurking where she was about to lay.

She didn't encounter anything sharper than the briars. Joseph lay close beside her. She whispered, "What in the world—"

"Shh. Listen."

Callie listened as intently as she could. At first she didn't hear anything, but then she began to make out soft sounds coming toward them. Somebody was walking through the woods but trying to be quiet about it . . . just as she and Joseph had done a short time earlier.

Men's voices murmured. Callie heard them but couldn't make out the words.

Putting her lips almost against Joseph's ear, she asked, "Do you think it's some of the Barlows?"

"Could be. We could have set off some kind of alarm coming in."

"Can they track us?"

"I don't know."

Callie's heart slugged in her chest. She had been part of more gunfights than she could remember in the movies . . . but not a one of them had been real. The thought that in a few minutes, somebody might be shooting at her and actually trying to kill her was enough to make her stomach feel unsettled and her blood race crazily in her veins.

Maybe she shouldn't have insisted on coming out here with her brother, after all.

But at the same time, if Joseph was about to be in trouble, she was glad she was here and might be able to help him.

During the dangerous encounters the day before, she hadn't had time to think about what was going on. She had reacted largely out of instinct. The tension she felt now, bordering on sickness, was worse.

Then, suddenly, the footsteps crunching on pine needles were close. Just on the other side of the briar thicket, in fact.

Somebody hissed a warning sound, and the steps stopped.

"Careful, Norm," a man said in a half-whisper. "They's supposed to be a tripwire somewhere around here."

"I see it! It's right there. See?"

"Good eye, Jimmy," the first man said.

"Reckon there's more than that?" another man asked. So there were three of them, at least.

The use of the names Norm and Jimmy told Callie something else, too. These weren't the Barlows. Just the opposite, in fact.

The Wolvertons had come to call.

Callie glanced over at Joseph and could tell from his expression that he had realized the same thing. He nodded to her. She mouthed the words *What are they doing here?* He shrugged and shook his head.

If they kept quiet and waited, maybe they would find out.

In the distance, the lawn mower's engine cranked and caught. It raced for a second and then settled back to a more normal rate as Julie eased off on the choke. Callie could tell by the way the sound rose and fell that Julie had driven the mower out of the storage shed and was moving around on it. The pitch changed again as the girl engaged the blades.

This time when the Wolvertons spoke, they raised their voices somewhat, as if no longer worried about being overheard.

"There she goes. Lord have mercy, it just ain't right a girl that pretty has to be a dang Barlow!"

"Take it easy, Jimmy. It don't matter how pretty Julie Barlow is. She ain't the reason we're here."

"She's the reason poor Tommy's in the hospital, though,

Earl," the third man said.

It must have been Tom Wolverton who laid down his bike, Callie thought. So the wreck hadn't killed him, at least not yet, but there was no telling how badly he was injured.

"The reason Tom's in the hospital is because he let Julie Barlow suck up to him in the first place," Earl said. "He should've knowed that little tramp was up to somethin' when she first came around. You can't trust none of those Barlows."

"I tried to tell him that, Earl." That was Jimmy again. "But you know Tommy. She batted them blue eyes at him and claimed she wanted to make peace betwixt the families, and he just ate it up with a spoon. I tried to tell him—"

"Shut up," Earl said. "Water under the bridge. We just gotta get that thumb drive back."

"They've copied it by now." That gloomy voiced comment came from Norman Wolverton. "Could've copied it a dozen times. Probably stored it in the cloud, too."

"Maybe. But it ain't worth anything anymore if they've done that. Why go to all the trouble of stealin' it in the first place if you're just gonna make sure it don't give you any leverage?"

Callie and Joseph looked at each other again. There was a lot of information flowing here, and Callie struggled to take it all in and digest it. One thing seemed certain, though.

Julie Barlow had lied to them the day before about why she was on the run from the Wolvertons.

Earl went on, "Whatever they've done, our next step is to get our hands on that drive. Nobody's in the house except Evelyn. We'll get in there while Julie's around on the other side, and she won't even know what's goin' on. Her mama won't give us no trouble. We make her give us the drive, and then we get out."

"I sure would like to settle the score with that Julie," Jimmy said.

"Yeah, well, the last score-settlin' we tried to do didn't work out so well, did it?"

Norman said, "Who knew some gal from California could fight like a wildcat?"

Callie knew they were talking about how they had ambushed her in her room at the lodge the night before. From the sound of it, that had been a simple attempt to settle the grudge they had against her and Joseph for rescuing Julie, nothing more.

The Wolvertons' foray against the Barlows today was part of a deeper game, a game that Julie evidently had been playing as well.

"Wait just a minute more," Earl said. "Lemme check with Sonny."

Callie heard a familiar but incongruous sound and realized that Earl had just sent a text message on a phone. A minute or so went by, then there was a faint chime to indicate that he'd gotten a reply.

"Lou and Charlie are still at the store in town," Earl said. "Sonny's got his eye on their pickup, so they can't head back this way without him knowin' it. He'll warn us if they do." Earl grunted. "We'll be in and outta there long before they can get back, anyway. Come on."

The stealthy footsteps resumed. Callie heard a brief pause

and wondered if that was because the three men were step-
ping carefully over that tripwire. It must have been, because
then the steps went on toward the house.

Joseph pushed himself up onto hands and knees and
moved so he could see around the thicket. Callie followed his
example. The Wolvertons were about forty feet away, stalking
through the woods toward the house. Two of them carried ri-
fles, while the third had a pump shotgun cradled in his hands.
All three wore work clothes and had ball caps on their heads.

In the distance on the far side of the house, the lawn mower
still rumbled.

The three Wolvertons broke out of the woods and ran toward the house. Callie and Joseph looked at each other for a
second, then Joseph said, "Stay here. I mean it, Callie."

"I hear you."

He nodded, stood up, reached to the small of his back and
drew the Browning Hi-Power from the holster there. Then he
started toward the house as well, weaving quickly through the
trees.

Callie climbed to her feet, reached under her shirt, and
gripped the Smith & Wesson 9mm. As she eased it from the
holster, she told herself that she wasn't breaking a promise.
When Joseph had told her to stay here, she had replied that
she heard him.

But she hadn't promised to do it.

She swallowed hard and went after him.

CHAPTER 19

By the time Callie reached the edge of the trees, the Wolvertons were no longer in sight. Joseph was angling toward the back of the house. Some instinct must have warned him that she was following, because he glanced over his shoulder, widened his eyes at her, and waved with the hand that wasn't holding the gun, indicating that she should go back.

She gave a stubborn shake of her head and kept coming. She moved as lightly as she could, but she heard her footsteps thudding on the ground. They sounded incredibly loud to her.

Joseph stopped at the rear corner of the house and pressed his back to the wall of the screened-in porch. He gestured urgently at Callie again, but this time he motioned her toward him, instead of back toward the woods. She hurried to join him and flattened herself against the wall, too.

"I won't waste my breath asking what you're doing here," he whispered.

"Where'd the Wolvertons go?"

"They're inside, I guess. The last I saw of them through the trees, they were heading for the back porch here."

He turned and leaned out a little to steal a glance around the corner. Callie did likewise. A couple of concrete steps led up to a screen door that opened onto the rear porch. That was the screen door they had heard open and close, the one Julie had used when she left the house to get the lawn mower out.

The mower still hummed on the other side of the house.

"What was all that about a thumb drive?" Callie asked.

"I have no idea. Something that has some bearing on the rivalry between the two families, I suppose. But it's nothing to do with why we're here."

"Then why *are* we here, with guns in our hands, instead of lying low in the woods?"

"That's exactly where you should be—" Joseph began.

A woman screamed inside the house. An instant later, a gun crashed. Callie jumped involuntarily at the sound. Hard on the heels of the shot, a man yelled curses. Rapid footsteps pounded the floor.

"Stay back," Joseph snapped at Callie, then wheeled around the corner with the Browning held in a two-handed grip. Despite his order, she followed him and stepped out in time to see three men burst out of the house's back door and lunge across the porch. The one in the lead slapped the screen door open and ignored the steps, bounding all the way to the grass at the bottom of them. He lost his balance when he landed and went to one knee, but recovered quickly and scrambled to his feet.

Joseph aimed the Browning at him and called, "Hold it!"

Callie cried, "Joseph, look out!" as one of the other men appeared at the top of the steps and leveled the shotgun he held. Callie gripped the S&W like she would have on a gun range and aimed above the man's head. She triggered twice.

The gun didn't have a lot of kick, but enough to force her arm up some as the shots blasted. The bullets ripped through the screen at the top of the door and caused the shotgunner to jerk backward. When he did, the weapon discharged with a dull boom, but the buckshot sprayed harmlessly high in the air.

The man who'd been first out of the house still clutched the rifle he had carried in. He tried to raise it and bring it to bear on Joseph, who shouted another warning at him. "Don't!"

Before either of them could fire, the zero turn mower with Julie Barlow on it roared around the house's far corner and zipped toward them, traveling at its top speed. Julie had both steering levers gripped in her left hand and pressed them forward together to keep the mower going reasonably straight.

In her right hand she held a revolver, and flame gushed from its barrel as she fired two shots.

The man with the rifle twisted, dropped his weapon, and staggered as blood welled from a hole in his upper right arm. He yelled, "I'm hit!"

The shotgunner had pumped another round into the chamber. Joseph leaped aside and rammed his shoulder into Callie, knocking her backward off her feet. The buckshot ripped through the air where they'd been standing an instant earlier.

The shotgunner and the third man leaped over the steps to the ground. The third man grabbed the arm of the one Julie had wounded and urged him into a run. They all dashed toward the trees at the rear of the property. Julie used both hands on the levers to jerk the mower into a tight turn and went after them, a backwoods valkyrie on a zero-turn instead of a winged steed. She steered with one hand again as the revolver boomed.

The fleeing Wolvertons didn't slow down or even break stride as they vanished into the woods.

Callie and Joseph lay there and watched the bizarre scene. Callie didn't know about her brother, but she was pretty shaken up by what had just happened. Her pulse was pounding, and she couldn't seem to get quite enough air into her lungs. She was only vaguely aware of hearing the screen door open and close again.

Then footsteps sounded nearby and she looked up to see a tall, bulky figure looming over them. She saw a thatch of graying chestnut hair, a mustache of the same shade, and the broad, muscular shoulders that stretched the khaki work shirt the man wore.

Callie also saw the twin muzzles of the double-barreled shotgun he pointed at them, and even as she realized why he looked familiar, he growled, "Who in blazes are you two, and gimme one good reason I shouldn't blow your heads off!"

"Daddy, don't shoot them!"

That shrill cry came from Julie, who had turned the mower around and was rolling toward them now.

Larry Don Barlow lowered the shotgun a little as he stepped back, but he kept it pointed in the general direction of Callie and Joseph as he said, "Don't worry, Julie honey. I won't kill 'em . . . yet."

◆ ◊ ◆

Five minutes later, Callie and Joseph sat side by side on a love seat in the big living room inside the Barlow house. Larry Don Barlow was across from them in an armchair not far from the impressive fireplace. Julie and her mother Evelyn, an attractive middle-aged blonde from whom Julie obviously had gotten her looks, were on a sofa to Callie and Joseph's left.

Larry Don had the shotgun resting across his lap, still handy but no longer pointing at Callie and Joseph. The Browning and the S&W he had taken away from them were on a small table next to the armchair.

Even though Callie and Joseph had been marched into the house at gunpoint, southern hospitality still had to be observed. Evelyn had brought glasses of iced tea for them and set the glasses on coasters on the coffee table in front of the love seat. She wasn't satisfied until Callie and Joseph had tasted the drinks and declared them to be delicious.

"We might as well get down to business," Larry Don said. "You're here to take me back to Corpus Christi, aren't you? You work for Bucko Corcoran?"

"You have us mixed up with somebody else," Joseph said. "We're just here to check out the retirement home—"

"You're a private investigator," Larry Don interrupted.

Callie said, "Private detectives can have grandfathers, too, can't they? Honestly, do you think Joseph would have dragged his sister along if we weren't in Hackberry on family business?"

"You're not a normal sister," Julie said. "You're like an action movie star. It didn't take long at all on the computer to figure that out." The girl shook her head. "I'm sorry, Callie. I really do appreciate the way you two helped me yesterday. I might not be alive now if you hadn't. But I know now that you're here plotting against my family."

"That's not true! We risked our lives again to help you to-day—"

"By charging in with guns," Larry Don said. "If you weren't looking for trouble, why were you carrying?"

"The two of us being armed doesn't prove anything," Joseph insisted. "You know better than that. Texas has constitutional carry now. *Lots* of people are armed, all the time."

"Most folks don't go skulkin' through the woods and sneaking up on somebody else's house, though."

Larry Don had a point there, Callie thought. And of course, he was right to be suspicious. Apprehending him as a fugitive was exactly why she and Joseph were here.

Unfortunately, *they* were the ones who'd been apprehended.

And for their trouble, they might wind up in shallow graves somewhere deep in the woods.

Joseph didn't seem bothered by that prospect. He sounded as cool and confident as ever as he said, "Look, from what I've seen, you could use some help, Mr. Barlow. It appears that these Wolvertons have launched an all-out war against you and your family."

"What do you know about the Wolvertons?" Larry Don growled.

"That they're your enemies and will go to any lengths to destroy your family . . . including carrying out hate crimes and framing the Barlows for them."

In sudden anger, Larry Don slammed a fist down on the arm of the chair where he sat.

"That's exactly what they done! We'd never have anything to do with burnin' down a church or desecratin' a graveyard or any of those other things they made it look like we did. It's all Earl's doin'. Him and his brother Norm. They're the ringleaders of that bunch."

"You mean the whole Wolverton family?" Callie asked. Larry Don was distracted at the moment by his anger at the Wolvertons. Might as well keep him that way, she thought, so he couldn't start planning where to put those shallow graves.

Julie said, "It's not all of them. Mostly just Earl and Norman and a few of their cousins."

"Like Tom and Jimmy," Joseph said.

"And Sonny and Carl and Lucas," Larry Don added. "Probably more we don't know about." He scrubbed a hand over his face, then went on, "I don't know why I'm botherin' to tell y'all about this."

"Because we'd like to help you," Callie said. "We have a grudge against the Wolvertons ourselves, by this point." She summoned up a smile. "The enemy of my enemy is my friend, as the old saying goes."

"Well, we got enough friends." Larry Don shrugged. "It's hard to cross paths with scum like the Wolvertons without windin' up hatin' 'em, though, I'll give you that."

"The feud goes 'way back," Julie said. "My granddaddy and great-granddaddy were rival moonshiners to the Wolvertons. They'd bust up each other stills and tip off the revenue agents when the other bunch would be making a delivery run.

Things just got worse from there. Earl and Norman, they're the worst that's ever been, though."

"I wouldn't put anything past those two," Larry Don said. "Us Barlows, we mostly made 'shine and then got into growin' and sellin' weed, too." He grunted. "Although that's gonna be legal, too, before you know it, I'll bet. We stole cars and some other stuff . . . high-level electronics, mostly . . . and run a few houses where . . . well . . ."

Evelyn frowned and said, "Larry Don, there's no need to talk about such things in front of the child."

"I'm not a child, Mama," Julie protested, "and I know what goes on in those houses."

"We never dealt in heroin or cocaine," Larry Don continued. "We never cooked meth. The Wolvertons done those things, and worse. They've got connections down on the border, and they traffic folks all over the country. Women and little kids . . ." He shook his head, and another growl rumbled deep in his chest. "I'm not sayin' us Barlows are saints. Not hardly. With the exception of a few like my Evelyn here, and Julie, who I've tried to keep as far away from what we do as I can. But we're not pure-dee evil like Earl and Norm Wolverton, I'll swear that on my own granddaddy's grave."

"I believe you," Joseph said. Callie didn't know if he meant it or not, but he certainly sounded sincere. "But you didn't manage to keep Julie out of the family business, did you?"

Julie looked embarrassed as her father frowned at her. "That was her own wild idea."

"It was a good idea," she defended herself. She looked at Callie and Joseph and went on, "I go to community college with Tom and Jimmy Wolverton. They're probably the smartest of the bunch. They know the most about computers, that's for sure. I overheard them talking about how they'd convinced Earl to let them run some sort of efficiency study on the family's dealings. They claimed they could show Earl ways to make the operation more profitable. But in order to do that, they had to put everything down and run it through the algorithms they'd come up with—"

"And that's what's on that thumb drive!" Callie exclaimed as she figured it out. "The whole Wolverton criminal empire."

Julie nodded. "That's right. I thought if I could get my hands on it, we could use it to get the Wolvertons to lay off of us, especially that business about trying to make folks think that we're white supremacists."

Evelyn said, "I just hate for anybody to think something like that about my family."

"We all do, dear," Larry Don said.

Callie and Joseph exchanged a quick glance. Larry Don had admitted that the Barlows were a bunch of bootlegging, dope-dealing, thieving whoremongers . . . but everybody had to draw the line *somewhere.*

Callie said to Julie, "So you played up to Tom Wolverton in order to steal that drive from him."

"Tom's always had a crush on me," Julie said, dropping her gaze to the floor for a second. "I think he had some sort of romantic, Romeo-and-Juliet notion about us. I didn't feel the same way, but I let him think that I did. I cozied up to him a little—"

Larry Don growled again.

"Don't worry, Daddy, I never let things get out of hand," Julie went on hurriedly. "But I let them take me on rides on their bikes, and yesterday I got Tom to bragging about what he'd done on the computer and he showed me the drive he'd stored everything on. I slipped it out of his pocket while we were . . . Well, I slipped it out of his pocket, and then tried to slip away from them, but they must've figured out what I'd done and came after me . . ." She shrugged. "And then you know everything that happened after that. The two of you saved my life."

"And helped you get away with the evidence that can destroy the Wolverton family," Joseph said. He looked at Larry Don. "It seems like that ought to be worth something."

He slitted his eyes at them. "You mean, like not killin' a couple of blasted bounty hunters?"

Callie said, "One thing Sheriff Whitfield told us about you, Mr. Barlow. You're not a murderer."

Larry Don heaved a sigh. "No, I don't reckon I am. But I'm not goin' back to Corpus with you, either, no matter what you did to help my little girl. I suppose I'll have to leave for real this time."

"Oh, no, honey," Evelyn said, leaning forward with an anxious expression on her face. "I don't want you to go."

"You don't want me to go to prison, either."

"Well, no, of course not."

"I don't understand," Callie said. "Does Sheriff Whitfield *know* that you're hiding out here at home?"

Larry Don shook his head. "I'm sure he suspects, but he's showed up two or three times, unannounced, to take a look around, and each time I've been deep enough in the woods that he never came close to finding me."

"You have somebody inside the sheriff's department tipping you off," Joseph said.

"That's right. Despite everything that's happened lately, all the things that've been blamed on us that we didn't have anything to do with, the Barlows still have plenty of friends in these parts."

Evelyn said, "When the sheriff came out, we never demanded that he have a search warrant. That made it look like we weren't worried about him finding Larry Don, because Larry Don wasn't here."

"But surely he knows what's really going on," Callie said. "Anybody who's ever seen a movie or TV show would know."

"Things that seem obvious on the TV screen aren't always that obvious in real life," Larry Don said. "Anyway, Howard and I played high school ball together. He wouldn't let that stop him from arrestin' me in a second if we came face to face. He's honest as the day is long. But at the same time, he ain't gonna dig too deep into things he don't want to find out. If you folks were from around here, you'd understand things like that."

"We understand," Joseph said. "The question is, what happens now?"

Don't put him on the spot like that, Callie thought, but maybe Joseph figured they had played this situation out for as long as they could.

"Like I said, I'll just have to leave," Larry Don replied.

"Evelyn and Julie and the boys have been telling folks that I'm workin' in West Texas, so I'll probably head out there. I really did work in the oil and gas fields for a while when I was a young man. Thought I didn't want to get into the family business. But it drew me back eventually. I still know a few old boys out in Odessa, though, who can help me lie low for a while."

"And Callie and me?"

Evelyn said, "You'll be our guests for a few days, until we know for sure that Larry Don is safe." She smiled. "It'll be nice to have some company."

The phone in Larry Don's shirt pocket buzzed. He took it out, looked at the display, and frowned.

"It's Chip," he said. "Shouldn't those boys have been back by now?"

As Larry Don answered the call, Callie said quietly to Julie, "Who's Chip?"

"My little brother Charles. Him and my other little brother Louis went into Hackberry earlier today."

Callie nodded. She remembered that one of the Wolvertons—Earl, she thought it was—had mentioned something about somebody called Sonny keeping an eye on "Lou and Charlie", obviously Julie's brothers.

A torrent of profanity suddenly burst out of Larry Don. He pulled the phone away from his ear, stared at it, and then acted for a second as if he were about to slam it to the floor. He stopped himself and looked up at his wife. Callie saw something on his face that she hadn't expected to see.

Fear.

"My lands, Larry Don," Evelyn said as she stood up and started toward him. "What in the world was *that* about?"

"I'm sorry for the language, honey," Larry Don replied in a hollow voice.

"But what did Chip say?"

"It wasn't Chip." Larry Don dragged in a breath and looked stricken. "It was Earl Wolverton. He and his bunch have the boys."

Chapter 20

Evelyn let out a short, terrified cry. Larry Don set the shotgun aside on the floor and stood up to go to her. She came up into his arms, which he folded around her as he said, "Don't you worry about it, honey. We'll get 'em back just fine. Those no-account Wolvertons wouldn't do anything to hurt 'em. Even as stupid as that bunch is, they know better than that."

"You don't believe that," Evelyn said, clearly distraught. She lifted her head to look up into her husband's face. "What did Earl say?"

Callie saw a little muscle jumping in Larry Don's cheek because his jaws were clenched so tight. For a moment, he couldn't speak, then he said, "He threatened to send the boys back to us one piece at a time unless we give 'em back that thumb drive and destroy any copies we made of it."

"We haven't made any copies," Julie said. "But how likely are they to believe that? How can we convince them?"

"Earl said they were willin' to trade," Larry Don went on. "Chip and Lou for the drive. He said . . ." Larry Don stopped and drew in a deep breath. "He said we'd make the swap at Froggy's tonight, in the dance hall."

Julie was on her feet, too. "Don't trust those Wolvertons, Daddy," she urged. "They'll try to trick you and double-cross you some way."

"Shoot, girl, you think I don't know that?" Larry Don asked as he looked over his wife's shoulder at their daughter. "But what else can I do? I got to go along with what they want. They've got your brothers."

"I know that." Julie sounded as miserable as she looked. "I just hate to let those blasted Wolvertons win—"

"Maybe we can help you," Joseph said.

That unexpected suggestion made everyone else in the room, including Callie, look at him in surprise. Larry Don frowned and asked, "What are you talkin' about, mister?"

"I assume there's going to be a dance at Froggy's tonight, and that's why the Wolvertons picked it for the exchange?"

"Yeah," Larry Don said. "The usual Friday night dance. Always has live music and folks come from miles around for it. B.J. Sawyer and the Lavaca River Boys are supposed to be there tonight, I think. Just what is it you figure you could do?"

Joseph didn't answer the question directly. Instead he said, "Did Earl give you some time to think it over?"

"Yeah, he said he'd call back in an hour, and if I was agreeable, we'd work out the details then."

Joseph nodded. "All right, he's probably going to insist that you turn over the thumb drive first, and more than likely he'll want you to give it to him personally. Then he'll signal the other members of his family who are working with him to release your boys."

Julie said, "More than likely, he'll tell the others to kill Chip and Lou."

The blunt statement drew another soft cry from Evelyn and a glare from Larry Don.

"What you need," Joseph said, "are some allies there who can locate the rest of the Wolvertons and your sons and step in to free them."

"That way I could double-cross Earl." Larry Don was starting to look interested.

"That's too risky," Evelyn protested. "We need to cooperate with them."

As if he hadn't heard her, Larry Don said, "There's no way we can pull that off. The Wolvertons know every member of our family, just like we know all of theirs." He shook his head. "Both sides grew up in the same small town and the same county. Everybody knows everybody else."

"They don't know my sister and me," Joseph said.

Callie had suspected that was where he was going with this conversation. She said, "Hold on a minute. The Wolvertons *do* know who we are. They've seen us three times, remember?"

Joseph held up a finger. "They've seen us at high speed, in another vehicle, while they were trying to ram us with their truck and I was trying to shoot them." A second finger went up. "Then last night in your room at the lodge, where the lights were off, and then in the parking lot, and again, there was a lot going on." He lifted a third finger. "And then today, and once again, gunplay was involved and everybody was moving fast. My point is, they've never gotten a good, long look at us."

"It still seems like a stretch to bet multiple lives on the hope that they wouldn't recognize us."

"Well," Joseph said, "I was thinking that if we do this, we could take steps to make it even less likely they'd recognize us . . ."

Callie felt ridiculous. She looked it, too, and she said as much as she gazed at herself in the mirror in Evelyn Barlow's bedroom.

"Oh, no, darlin', you look good. Just a little on the, well . . ."

"Trashy side?" Callie suggested. "Isn't that the title of some country-and-western song?"

Her dark hair was tucked up under a blond, curly wig right out of the Big Hair Eighties. She wore her own jeans, but she'd changed her shirt for a turquoise long-sleeved number with spangles and pearl snaps. It was a little tight, but she compensated for that by leaving the top two snaps undone. Intricately patterned, sharp-toed crocodile skin boots had replaced her scuffed, comfortable running shoes.

"I wore that get-up to a few New Year's Eve costume parties," Evelyn said. "But honestly, it's not much different from what I wore all the time, forty years ago when I was a young woman. We all dressed like that then."

Callie turned a little and studied herself from another angle. "Maybe," she allowed.

"Oh, I know all you hippies and beach bunnies down there

in Corpus never dressed like that, and goodness knows, nobody in California would be caught dead looking like you do now, but honestly, I like it."

"If you say so." Callie pushed at the wig to fluff it up a little more . . . as if it needed fluffing up.

She was sure of one thing: it wasn't likely anyone who had only caught glimpses of her the way she normally looked would recognize her in this disguise.

"I think you look great," Julie said from where she sat on the edge of her parents' bed. "I'm not sure I'd know you, especially in a smoky dance hall."

She got up when a knock sounded on the door and went to open it. Joseph stood there in jeans, cowboy shirt, brown felt Stetson, and ostrich-hide boots. He nodded, pinched the hat's brim, and said, "Howdy, ma'am."

Julie laughed, the sound a welcome counterpoint to the tension they were all feeling. Callie looked at her brother and said, "You're an insult to cowboys everywhere."

"But I look different, don't I?"

"You do, at that," she admitted. She looked at Julie. "You're sure this is the way people dress at these dances?"

"Some do. Some just wear regular clothes, but a lot of them like to get gussied up. Over here in East Texas, it's more country than Western, but you'll find plenty of Western influences, too. The two of you stand together."

They did so, and Callie felt distinctly awkward. But Julie nodded and went on, "I'd never know you."

"We need to be able to recognize the Wolvertons, though," Joseph said. "You've said that the families went to school with each other. Do you have any yearbooks that would have their pictures in them?"

Julie nodded. "I should. Why don't you go back downstairs, and I'll see what I can find?"

Callie, Joseph, and Evelyn went down to the living room, where they found Larry Don sitting in the same armchair, brooding with his chin propped on a fist as he leaned on one of the arms.

He sat up straight and studied Callie and Joseph, moving his gaze from pointed boot toes to hats and back again. Callie had donned a light-brown hat that was held on the mass of curly blond hair by a rawhide strap under her chin.

"Well, you two look mighty different, I have to give you that," he said after a moment. "This plan of yours might not be totally crazy, Kingfisher."

"I hope not," Joseph said. "I'll hang around near the dance hall's entrance, and if any of the Wolvertons come in, that'll be my signal to drift out to the parking lot and see if I can find the others . . . and your sons."

"There's no guarantee they'll even bring Chip and Lou with them," Larry Don said. "No guarantee those boys are even still alive."

"Oh, honey, don't say that," Evelyn objected. "We . . . we have to keep our hopes up."

Larry Don nodded. "Yeah, maybe. The Wolvertons are evil sons o' guns, but not all of them are stupid. Earl isn't. He knows that if he hurt those boys, it'd be scorched earth from there on out. We wouldn't stop until every last Wolverton was dead."

Callie remembered things she had read about famous Texas feuds. She didn't doubt that Larry Don meant what he said, every word of it.

He went on, "They've been pushed into a corner by what Julie did, or they might not have made such a desperate move—"

He stopped short as footsteps sounded at the top of the stairs. Julie came down with several large books in her hands, as well as some sheets of paper.

"These school yearbooks have Tom, Jimmy, Sonny, Lucas, and Carl in them," she said as she placed the books on the coffee table. She held up the papers and went on, "Earl and Norman are quite a bit older, so I found some pictures of them on the Internet and printed them out."

Larry Don grunted. "What are those pictures, mug shots from the county jail website?"

"Well . . . yes, actually. They've both been arrested several times."

"Haven't we all?" Larry Don said wearily.

Joseph and Callie sat down on the love seat again and began studying the photographs Julie pointed out to them in the yearbooks, as well as the printed images. Earl Wolverton was actually a rather handsome man, with curly dark hair and a cleft chin. Callie had never noticed that during the brief shootout earlier. His younger brother Norman was much more heavyset, with a round face and thinning dark hair slicked down over his scalp.

The other Wolvertons who were approximately Julie's age all bore a family resemblance. Looking at them, Callie thought she would have pegged them as a family of backwoods criminals, but maybe that wasn't really fair on her part, she told herself, since she already knew what they were.

"We know Sonny is the one who was watching your boys in town," Joseph said as he tapped a photo in one of the yearbooks. "Earl mentioned that to Norman and Jimmy. So he's probably one of the group that grabbed him."

"If Sonny was there, then Carl and Lucas were, too," Larry Don said.

"Those boys are like peas in a pod," Evelyn added. "You'd almost think they were triplets, the way they act, instead of cousins."

"Whatever they are, they're dangerous. I don't see Earl trustin' those three to keep up with prisoners by themselves, though. He'd have Norm watchin' over them, and might have a few more of the family around close by, too." Larry Don looked intently at Joseph and Callie. "No matter what, the two of you are gonna be outnumbered, maybe by a lot."

"That's why I intend to rely more on guile than brute force," Joseph said. "Ideally, we'll be able to distract the boys' captors and free them before the Wolvertons know what's going on."

"That'll be a nice job . . . *if* you can pull it off." Larry Don fell silent for a moment, then said, "What are the chances that Earl might play it straight and turn those boys loose if I give him what he wants?"

"You'd know the answer to that a lot better than I would, Mr. Barlow. You're the one who's been their rival for all these years."

"I just worry about doin' the wrong thing—"

"You should just stop thinking that, Larry Don," Evelyn said with unexpected force. "You've been the leader of this family ever since your daddy stepped down, and you've never steered us wrong."

"I managed to get caught with a truckload of hot cars in Corpus," Larry Don pointed out with a faint, grim smile.

"That was just bad luck. Anybody can have some bad luck sneak up on them every now and then. You can't do anything about that. But your instincts have always been trustworthy, you know that. What do they tell you now? Are the Wolvertons planning some sort of treachery?"

"Every bone in my body tells me that they are."

Evelyn reached over and patted his knee. "Well, then, there you go, honey. You know what you've got to do."

"I reckon. Thanks for that." Larry Don returned his attention to Callie and Joseph. "All right. I'll be there for the meet with Earl at Froggy's. You two see if you can find the rest of the Wolvertons and get the boys away from 'em. If they're safe, you call me and let me know." A bleak expression settled over his face. "Then I'll deal with Earl."

"You can't kill him," Evelyn said. "That'd start a war, too, just the same as if any harm came to our boys."

"Maybe. Maybe not. Not as long as we've got that computer file that could bring their whole operation crashin' down. You know Earl and Norm have always been loose cannons. The rest of the family might not be that upset if somethin' were to happen to them and the rest of the firebrands they pull in with them. Rivalry or not, as long as we're all still in business, we're all still makin' money."

That made sense to Callie, even though she had no practical knowledge of organized crime, only what she had gleaned from movies and TV and books. But Joseph was nodding slowly, too, as if he agreed with what Larry Don was saying.

"Speaking of money . . ." Joseph said.

Larry Don frowned at him. "Yeah, you're a private detective, aren't you? I suppose you want to get paid for your part in this."

"Not exactly."

"Well, then, what *do* you want?"

Joseph looked levelly at him and said, "I think you can probably figure that out."

Larry Don continued to glare at him for a long moment before finally saying, "You've got to be kidding."

"I think it's only fair," Joseph said. "My sister and I help you get your boys back safe and sound, and you come peacefully with us back to Corpus Christi and face whatever's waiting for you there."

"No!" Evelyn cried. "That's not right."

Julie was on her feet, scowling at Joseph and Callie. "I thought you two were on our side," she said. "You helped me—"

"Because it looked like the right thing to do, not knowing anything about the situation. We didn't know we'd be risking our lives by getting mixed up in a war between two crime families."

"You say that like we're . . . we're gangsters or something! Like this is . . . Chicago instead of East Texas!"

Joseph shrugged. "Crime is crime, no matter where it is. But here's the thing. We're not trying to bring down your family. We have no interest in whatever activities you're involved in, legal or not." He looked at Larry Don. "All we were hired to do is bring you back."

Callie's heart pounded. It seemed to her that Joseph was practically begging for that shallow grave in the woods.

Larry Don said, "What'll you do if I don't go along with your idea?"

Joseph spread his hands and said, "What can we do? We're in no position to force you to come with us. Oh, I suppose we could tell the sheriff that you're here, but by the time he could do anything about it, you'd be gone again. Anyway, I don't think Sheriff Whitfield would be in a big hurry to believe us. We're outsiders, after all."

"That's right," Larry Don said heavily. "Nobody'd miss you if anything was to happen to you."

Evelyn shook her head. "Oh, Larry Don, I don't like it when you talk like that. You know you're not—"

"Excuse me, Mrs. Barlow," Callie broke in. Joseph shot a warning glance at her, as if to say that he didn't know what she was doing but that she ought to let him handle this. But she went on, "Like my brother said, we helped your daughter yesterday because it was the right thing to do. We stepped in this afternoon for the same reason, when we could have stayed hidden in the woods and let the Wolvertons do whatever they came to do. And tonight . . . we'll do our best to help rescue your sons because it's the right thing to do."

"You will?" Larry Don snapped.

Callie nodded. "That's right. We'll help you. No strings attached."

"That's no way to do business," Joseph said.

"Maybe not. But I don't like those Wolvertons. And I don't like them threatening a couple of teenagers, either."

Joseph sat in silence for a long moment, as if pondering what she'd said, and then he began to nod slowly.

"Callie is right," he said with a shrug. "We've picked our side, and we're going to stick with it, no matter what you decide to do, Mr. Barlow. Let's get your sons back first and then figure it out."

Larry Don squinted at them. "Is this some sort of trick?"

"No, sir. We have a plan, and I think we should follow it. Everything else can wait until your sons are safe and you've settled things, at least for the moment, with the Wolvertons."

Larry Don jerked his head in a nod and said, "All right, you've got a deal. We get the boys back, and then we'll talk about it some more."

Julie folded her arms across her chest and said, "There's just one thing we haven't settled yet."

"What's that, dear?" her mother asked.

"I'm coming along tonight, too . . . and I don't want to hear any argument about it, Daddy."

CHAPTER 21

Larry Don put his hands on his knees and rose to his feet to stare at his daughter in a stern manner.

"Well, you're *gonna* get an argument about it, whether you want to hear one or not," he declared.

"Listen, Daddy, the boys wouldn't be in danger if it weren't for me and that crazy idea I had to steal that thumb drive."

"It *was* a pretty foolish thing to do," Evelyn said. "But you were just trying to help the family, dear. We know that."

"We also know you're not goin' anywhere near Froggy's tonight," Larry Don said.

Julie glared at him. "You can't stop me. I'm a grown woman. I can go to a dance hall if I want to."

"I don't care how old you are, you're my daughter and you live under my roof. That means what I say, goes. And I say you're not goin'."

"How do you plan on stopping me?" she shot back at him, defiantly.

"How about I just lock you in your room?"

Julie flipped her hair. "I'll climb out the window. One of the limbs of that old pecan tree is easy to reach. I ought to know, I did it plenty of times when I was in high school, and you never had any idea I was sneaking out, either of you."

"Oh, Julie," her mother said.

Joseph said, "I don't like to interfere in family matters—"

"Then maybe you shouldn't," Larry Don interrupted to tell him.

Undaunted, Joseph went on, "But Julie might come in helpful tonight. She knows all the Wolvertons. She could watch for them, too, and give us the high sign if any of them come in. As long as she stays inside the dance hell, she ought to be all right. Froggy's is neutral ground, right?"

"Yeah, it's supposed to be," Larry Don admitted with obvious reluctance. "But with the way things have been going lately, I don't trust them to honor that tradition. Back when Edgar Wolverton—that's Earl and Norm's father—was running things, he kept a tight enough rein on the whole family that nobody would've dared try that stunt of framing us for hate crimes. And before that, when old Enoch was still in charge, they wouldn't have even dreamed of doin' such a thing. The Wolvertons are outlaws, sure. So are the Barlows. But those are the sort of dirty tricks lowdown, big-city criminals would do."

Callie wasn't sure but what Larry Don was just rationalizing his family history with that talk of honor. From what she had heard of the Barlows, their activities were pretty shady and had been for a long time. But thinking of themselves as backwoods Robin Hoods probably helped Larry Don and his relatives sleep better at night.

"They won't try anything at Froggy's," Julie insisted. "They'd be afraid to. Everybody loves Froggy."

"I still wouldn't put anything past that bunch."

Callie could tell that Julie was going to keep arguing, and that wasn't getting them anywhere. She said, "Listen, Mr. Barlow, what if I give you my word that I'll keep Julie right with me and won't let anything happen to her? Like my brother said, having her there might come in handy, and not just for keeping an eye out for the Wolvertons." Callie smiled. "She can also give me tips on how to blend in. After spending years in California, I'm not sure I can do that in East Texas anymore."

"Yeah, you look good," Julie said with a smile of her own, "but you might ruin everything by asking for a Pink Moscato Lemonade at the bar. Then *everybody* would know that you're not from around these parts!"

Larry Don still tried to look stern and grim, but Callie thought she spotted a faint smile tugging at his lips under the mustache. Evelyn smiled, too, and Joseph chuckled.

"That's exactly what she'd do," he said.

"Hey, I haven't forgotten completely what it's like to be a Texas girl!" Callie protested.

Larry Don raised his hands, palms out. "All right, all right," he said. "You can go, Julie, but I'm gonna be keepin' an eye on you, too. You stay where you'll be safe, you hear me? You try to go sneakin' off, I'll catch you, and you'll be sorry. You're not so big I can't still put you over my knee and paddle you."

Julie made a face and stuck her tongue out at him.

"Kinda proves my point, don't it?" Larry Don said.

◆ ◇ ◆

When they were at Froggy's the day before, Callie hadn't really noticed that there was a large, gravel-paved parking lot on the far side of the diner and the dance hall, extending well back from the road, past the cavernous, barn-like building.

That lot was more than half full when she and Joseph arrived there that evening, with Callie driving the Ram this time. In addition, people coming to dance were parked in front of the diner and in the Lazy Pines Motel lot. The dance hall had entrances on both sides, with signs that read *FROGGY'S LAZY PINES DANCE HALL* above them.

"Looks like a popular place for Friday evening get-togethers, all right," Joseph commented as they got out of the pickup. Callie left her cane in the truck. It didn't go with her disguise, so she figured she'd just have to do without it tonight. Her leg didn't ache much, and all the stiffness was gone.

"Everybody comes to Froggy's," she said. "Isn't that a book?"

"You're thinking of a play called *Everybody Comes to Rick's*," Joseph said. "They made a movie from it. Little thing called *Casablanca*. You may have seen it."

"Very funny. I don't think we're going to find Humphrey Bogart and Ingrid Bergman in there." Callie looked over at Joseph as he broke stride for a second. "Are you all right?"

"These boots pinch a little. I'm not used to them."

"Well, you'd better get used to them. We'll need to be out there boot-scootin' on the dance floor with everybody else, otherwise we'll stand out. And we don't want to draw attention from the wrong people."

Joseph nodded. "I know exactly who you mean."

They joined the throng of people paying a five dollar entrance fee to get in. Froggy must make good money on these dances, Callie thought. They paid up, and the man at the door stamped the back of their left hands so they could go in and out of the hall.

Most people were dressed casually, as Evelyn and Julie had said they would be, but some couples had gone to more trouble. Callie wouldn't have guessed that anybody still wore rhinestones on their clothes, but clearly, some did. At least three-fourths of the crowd wore cowboy hats, men and women alike. Fancy boots and tight jeans. Even a few shirts ornately decorated with glitter and fringe.

The air was surprisingly smoke-free, despite Julie's reference to a "smoky dance hall". The air was full of music, though, at the moment the mournful strains of George Strait's *Amarillo By Morning*. The song wasn't live; it came over the speakers hung among the rafters, above the purposely unfinished ceiling. The bandstand at the far end of the room was still empty at this point. B.J. Sawyer and the Lavaca River Boys had yet to put in an appearance.

The last plaintive notes of the George Strait song faded away and were replaced by an upbeat tune from some female singer Callie didn't recognize. She said to Joseph, "I'm not up to date on country music. Who's this?"

"I have no idea," he said. He nodded toward the couples already moving around on the dance floor. "Should we join them?"

"Not just yet." Callie nodded toward what appeared to be a snack bar to the left of the entrance. "Let's get something to drink, and find a good place to keep an eye on things."

"That's going to be more difficult than I expected, with entrances on both sides of the room."

"We may have to split up."

Joseph looked like he didn't care for that idea, but they were here to accomplish their objective and they had come this far, so neither of them wanted to back out now.

The snack bar had two dozen tables in front of it. A similar arrangement was set up on the far side of the room, near that entrance, Callie noted. She and Joseph got Dr Peppers and sat at one of the tables, looking around the big room.

"I'll stay here," Callie suggested. "You can sit at one of the tables on the other side. We ought to be able to see everybody who comes and goes."

"What if we spot one of the targets?"

Callie slid her phone from one of the hip pockets of her tight jeans and woke it up. She frowned as she looked at the display. "Doesn't look like very good service in here."

"I'm not surprised." Joseph tipped his head back slightly to look up at the rafters and roof. "The building is blocking reception. That's pretty common out here where service isn't that great to start with."

"I could try sending you a text anyway. It might go through." She shrugged. "Otherwise we'll just have to try to keep an eye on each other."

"Which is going to be difficult once the place gets really crowded."

"There's nothing else we can do. It's too late to back out now."

Joseph drank some of his Dr Pepper. "Who said anything about backing out? Look, there's Larry Don and Julie."

The two Barlows had just come in. Larry Don shook hands with several men. Lots of grinning and hand-shaking went on.

"Don't people around here know that he's a fugitive from the law?" Callie asked under her breath.

"Some probably do, but more than likely most don't. And a lot of the ones who do know won't care. To them, the Barlows are like . . . folk heroes, I imagine."

"Like Jesse James or Billy the Kid."

"Exactly."

Julie had broken away from her father. She came toward the snack bar, stood in line and bought a drink, and then sat down at one of the empty tables near Callie and Joseph without ever looking in their direction . . . at least not so that anyone would notice. They were all aware of each other's presence, though, Callie could tell.

At the far end of the room, musicians climbed onto the bandstand, bringing guitars and fiddles with them, except for one man who went to the drum kit that was already set up and an attractive young woman with long blond hair who positioned herself behind an electric keyboard.

"Looks like one of the Lavaca River Boys is a girl," Callie commented.

The pre-recorded music over the PA system ended. The band tuned their instruments and warmed up for several minutes, sounding as discordant as bands always did at those times. Then one of the guitarists stepped to a stand microphone and said, "Well, howdy out there, folks, and welcome to Froggy's!"

Enthusiastic whoops and applause welled up from the crowd.

"I'm B.J. Sawyer, and these are the Lavaca River Boys!"

More reaction from the crowd.

"We're here tonight to play for your listenin' and dancin' pleasure, and I don't know about you, but me and the boys intend to get right on down to business! So here's a tune made popular by the immortal Bob Wills . . . *San Antonio Rose!*"

The shouts of approval were almost loud enough to rattle the rafters.

Joseph leaned closer to Callie and said over the music, but quietly enough that the words wouldn't be overheard, "I'll go on over to the other side of the room. It looks like Larry Don is drifting in that direction."

Callie nodded. A lot of couples had started dancing as soon as the band began playing, but a large number of people were still just standing around talking and drinking soft drinks and beers from the snack bars. Larry Don was among them, moving slowly toward the far side of the room as Joseph had indicated, stopping frequently to talk to someone. He appeared to be totally at ease, but Callie knew that was just a pose.

Joseph stood up and walked away. A few moments later, Julie stood up at the table where she'd been sitting and moved over to join Callie.

With an apparent smile of welcome, Callie said, "Should we be sitting together?"

"Oh, shoot, nobody'll think anything of it," Julie said. "On Friday night, everybody is friends at Froggy's. You may not know somebody, but that doesn't mean they're a stranger. Anybody looking at us will just think we're talking."

"Well, that *is* all we're doing."

"You know what I mean, just shootin' the breeze. Hey, girls dance with girls sometimes. Nobody here cares."

"But you're not asking me to dance, are you?"

"Oh, no. Not that I wouldn't—"

"We can leave it at that," Callie said. "Any sign of our mutual friends?"

"They're no friends of mine," Julie said with a slight scowl. "But I know what you mean, and no, I haven't seen any of that bunch so far. I wish they'd go ahead and show up. The sooner they do, the sooner my brothers will be safe."

"Let's hope so," Callie said.

They sat there with their drinks, talking quietly, for what seemed like a long time to Callie but probably was no more than twenty or thirty minutes. Julie nodded toward a number of people on the dance floor and told Callie stories about them. Evidently Hackberry County was full of eccentrics who got up to bizarre, amusing antics at times.

Maybe most places were like that, Callie mused, except in the big towns, no one really knew their neighbors, wasn't aware of their struggles and triumphs. Their stories were theirs alone, and it was easy not to care.

Julie was telling Callie about a man whose hog had gotten loose from him and stampeded through a Wednesday night service at the Baptist Church when she stopped suddenly and leaned forward in her chair. A visible air of tension gripped her.

"What is it?" Callie asked.

"Earl Wolverton just came in," Julie said, "and he's headed for Daddy."

At the same time, a voice from behind Callie spoke loudly enough to be heard over the music, asking, "Callie Kingfisher, is that you in that get-up?"

CHAPTER 22

Callie jerked her head around and saw Felicity Prosper standing there with a bottle of beer in her hand. Felicity wore jeans, but they were expensive, designer ones, like her shoes and the elegant top she had on. She looked completely out of place among the Hackberry County folks, even the ones who'd gotten gussied up for the dance.

"It *is* you," Felicity went on. "I almost didn't recognize you in that hat and wig. I'm used to interviewing people in makeup and costume for movie roles, though, so I'm good at seeing through the surface effects. What are you doing here looking like that?" Felicity's eyes widened, as if something had just occurred to her. "Is this for a movie? Is that what's really going on?"

Callie wished she and Joseph were involved in something as harmless as a movie. She didn't know which way to look, so she turned her head back and forth. She wanted to shut up Felicity, because the TV personality clearly didn't care if anything she said was overheard, but at the same time, she wanted to get eyes on Earl Wolverton and see what he was doing. Julie was already starting to look anxious.

Callie stood up and took one last glance across the room. It was too crowded. She couldn't pick out Earl from the press of people between her and the other entrance. She turned to Felicity and said, "The question is, what are *you* doing here?"

"I was told that practically everyone who's anybody in this county shows up for these dances on Friday night," Felicity replied. "I'm hoping that includes Larry Don Barlow, the current head of that white supremacist crime family."

Callie saw Julie's lips tighten and hoped the girl wasn't about to erupt in anger at Felicity for repeating the scurrilous accusation.

Felicity noticed Julie, too, and went on, "Who's your lovely little friend?"

Before anybody had to answer that question, Josh Green, the young producer, pushed through the crowd and hurried toward them. As he came up, a little breathless, he said, "I found him, Felicity. He's over there on the other side of the room."

"Barlow?" Felicity asked sharply.

"Yeah. Just standing there, talking to some other guy, as big and bold as you please, not like he's a criminal at all!"

Julie stood up and began, "He's not—", stopping short when Callie glared at her.

Felicity didn't miss that. "What's going on here?" she asked. "Who are you? Are you connected with the Barlows?" She caught her breath as she stared at Julie. "Are you *one of them*?"

"Felicity, just back off," Callie snapped. She couldn't see Joseph or Larry Don or Earl Wolverton. There were too many people around the dance floor and gathered at the snack bars. It was too crowded in here, and Callie felt claustrophobic, a feeling that the loud music from the bandstand didn't help. Her nerves drew taut . . .

And suddenly she was falling again, plummeting helplessly through the air, and above her, reaching out a hand toward her, begging for help but getting farther and farther away, was her sister Vickie . . .

Callie stiffened and forced a deep breath into her lungs. She didn't have time for this now. She could always have a nervous breakdown later.

"I'm going to find your brothers," she told Julie. "Stay here."

Felicity grabbed her arm. "Wait a minute. Who are her brothers? What is this, Callie?"

Josh said with some urgency in his voice, "Felicity, we need to go confront the guy. Nick's got his camera ready. It'll be a great story!"

Callie jerked her arm loose from Felicity's grasp and headed for the door. She didn't look back to see if Julie was staying put, although she hoped the girl would do as she was told. She wasn't sure how she was going to find the younger Barlows and their kidnappers. The parking lot was big, and they might not even be in this lot but rather around on the other side of the building.

She had the images of the other Wolvertons frozen in her mind, though, so she'd just have to look around and see if she could spot them. She didn't think Norman or Jimmy would recognize her in this disguise, and the other Wolvertons had never laid eyes on her.

She hurried out into the warm, muggy night. People were still coming in, walking from their vehicles to the hall's entrance. Callie knew none of them would be her quarry. The men she was looking for would still be in a car or pickup or SUV, waiting for a signal from Earl that the prisoners should be released. *If* Earl wasn't going to try to pull a double-cross, that is.

The signal might well be an order to kill Chip and Lou Barlow, Callie thought, and the prospect chilled her blood a little despite the cloying warmth of the air around her.

She prompted a few angry exclamations by peering into vehicles were couples were making out before heading into the dance hall, but she didn't find the Wolvertons. She was torn between searching the entire parking lot or going on around to the other side. Maybe Joseph was already over there, she told herself. Maybe the whole thing was finished and the boys were safe, while she was wandering around out here futilely in the dark.

That thought had just gone through her mind when gunshots slammed inside the dance hall and people started to scream.

Joseph had his eye on Larry Don Barlow as the man slowly made his way across the dance hall toward him. Larry Don wore a jovial expression on his face, and plenty of hand-shaking and back-slapping went on along the way. Clearly, Larry Don was well-liked around here, despite his family's criminal activities.

Or maybe because of them, Joseph reflected. Crimes of the sort that the Barlows specialized in, crimes that catered to people's vices, usually existed because people *wanted* them to. That was why Prohibition had been such a spectacular failure, and then later, although not in such a dramatic fashion, the so-called War on Drugs.

If there was a market for something, good or bad, somebody was going to provide the supply. True, the Barlows had branched out into other things, such as car theft—which had gotten Larry Don caught—but their criminal organization was built on illegal booze.

That would make a lot of the citizens of Hackberry County consider Larry Don a friend. They wanted what he could provide. And there was probably a healthy amount of respect and even fear mixed in with their reactions to him. Nobody would want to get on the wrong side of the Barlows.

Except the Wolvertons. They didn't care, because they were even worse.

Joseph leaned against the wall near the snack bar. He had tried sitting at one of the tables, but he hadn't been able to see well enough from there. His height gave him a little advantage. Larry Don was tall, too, so it was easier to keep track of him.

Also easier to spot the man approaching from the entrance on the side of the hall toward the big parking lot. Joseph had studied the picture of Earl Wolverton intently enough that he recognized the newcomer immediately.

He wondered, briefly, if Callie had seen Wolverton come into the dance hall, too.

Larry Don had noticed his enemy, no doubt about that. The crowd parted around Earl—no liking there, but plenty of fear—and the two men confronted each other. With the music still booming out from the bandstand, Joseph had no hope of hearing what Larry Don and Earl were saying to each other, but it was obvious from their expressions and the tense way they stood that the conversation was far from a friendly one. Folks backed off and gave them room.

Joseph's job now was to slip out of the hall and locate the hostages while Larry Don stalled his adversary. If Callie had spotted Earl, there was a good chance she'd be doing the same thing on the other side of the building. Joseph hadn't wanted the two of them to split up, but the way things had turned out, there really wasn't anything better they could have done.

He hoped Callie would be careful, he thought as he went outside. He knew she could take care of herself, but she was much more accustomed to make-believe violence than the real thing.

The lot on this side of the building wasn't as full as the one on the other side, but plenty of vehicles were parked here anyway. Joseph weaved hurriedly through them, drawing some puzzled looks from people just arriving to go into the dance. He didn't have time to worry about whether he was attracting attention. The important thing was determining if the two captive Barlow boys were out here.

He had checked about half the vehicles in the lot when

several shots suddenly erupted inside the dance hall. Joseph stopped short where he was and turned his head to stare at the entrance as people began to spill out in panic. Then he broke into a run toward the doors.

Callie's first impulse was to hurry back into the dance hall and make sure Joseph was all right, but before she could do that, she spotted movement in the next aisle of parked vehicles and leaned around the cab of a pickup to see several figures hurriedly getting out of a dark SUV.

The three men hadn't thought to remove the bulb from the dome light, and as the yellow glow spread from inside the vehicle's cab, it washed over faces that Callie recognized.

Those were three of the Wolvertons. The young ones . . . Sonny, Carl, and Jimmy. They pulled guns from under their shirts and ran toward the entrance.

Callie wanted to follow them, maybe get the drop on them and disarm them before they could involve themselves with the trouble inside the building, but she also knew there was a chance that Chip and Lou Barlow were in that SUV. If she could free them, that might help defuse the violence more than anything else she could do. She circled the pickup and ran toward the SUV.

Before she reached it, the back door on the side facing her swung open and a thick-set figure stepped out. She couldn't see the man's face, but his shape matched that of Norman Wolverton. He waved an arm at her and ordered in a rumbling voice, "Get away from here, girl. This ain't no place for you."

"Norm, is that you?" Callie cried, making her voice sound upset. She had done very little actual acting in Hollywood, but she'd had a few speaking parts and that experience served her well now.

Norman Wolverton stepped closer, and Callie could hear the confusion in his voice as he began, "Who the blazes are—"

She kicked him in the groin.

Nothing fancy about it, just a swift strike with a pointed-toe boot where it would hurt the worst. Norm screamed and started to double over. Callie laced her fingers together and swung her clubbed hands at his jaw, putting her weight and momentum behind the blow. It landed cleanly, snapping his head to the side. His knees buckled. He fell onto them and then pitched forward. Callie had to hop backward nimbly to keep his senseless form from landing on her.

She hurried around him and leaned into the still-open door. "Chip! Lou! Are you in here?"

Muffled noises came from the cargo area in the back.

Callie sprang to that door and lifted it. A large, bulky some-thing under a blanket was moving around. Two somethings, actually. Callie jerked the blanket away and uncovered the two young men. They had strips of duct tape over their mouths, and their wrists were duct-taped behind them. More tape secured their ankles.

"Chip and Lou Barlow?" Callie asked. The muffled but en-thusiastic response from the two youngsters confirmed their identities.

Callie went on, "I'm a friend of your family," which was kind of true. "This is going to hurt."

She picked at one of the strips of tape until she'd loosened one end, then grabbed it and yanked. Chip or Lou, whichever boy it was, yelped in pain as the tape came off.

More shots from inside the dance hall punctuated the sound.

Callie reached behind him and tried to work loose the tape around his wrists. She couldn't get it loose, but she had come equipped with a folding knife and took it out of her pocket.

"Hold still," she said. "I don't want to cut you."

She sawed through the tape. The youngster gasped in relief as his arms came loose. Callie pressed the knife into his hands, but he fumbled it, probably because his fingers had no feeling in them from being secured too tightly for too long.

"When you get the feeling back in your hands, use the knife to finish freeing yourself and your brother," she told him. She spotted a roll of duct tape lying on the floor of the SUV's cargo area. She picked it up and stepped back to go to work on Norman Wolverton.

She pulled one arm behind his back and then the other, then wrapped the tape around and around his wrists several times. He was starting to make noises, but by the time he came around, she had him securely bound, hand and foot. She finished off the job by slapping a length of tape across his mouth so he couldn't yell for help.

"Ma'am, who *are* you?" The question came from one of the boys.

"Like I said, a friend of the family."

With that, Callie reached under her shirt, pulled the Smith & Wesson 9mm from the belly holster, and ran toward the dance hall, ignoring the occasional twinge of pain from her leg.

CHAPTER 23

Joseph had to fight against the mob of people trying to get out of the dance hall as he attempted to get back in. The gunfire had put an abrupt end to the music, and the bandstand was empty, Joseph saw as he finally stumbled through the doors. The Lavaca River Boys had beaten a fast retreat when the trouble started.

Some of the dancers, unable or too frightened to reach the exits, had turned over the tables in the snack bar area and crouched behind them, seeking whatever shelter they could find.

Earl Wolverton, with his left arm looped around Felicity Prosper's neck, dragged the TV reporter with him as he backed toward the bandstand. He had a Glock in his right hand and fired it at Larry Don Barlow, who rolled behind one of the overturned tables.

A few yards away, Josh Green lay sprawled on his belly with his arms over his head, as if that would protect him from bullets. Joseph didn't see Nick Baker, the cameraman and driver.

Larry Don had a gun in his hand, but he held his fire because Earl was using Felicity as a shield. Earl wasn't worried about harming innocents, though. He continued blasting away until the Glock was empty.

By then he had backed almost all the way to the bandstand. He pushed the button to drop the empty magazine from the pistol and reached for a fresh magazine with the same hand, intent on reloading without letting go of Felicity. No one was close enough to rush him while he was busy doing that, and although Felicity struggled feebly in his grip, it didn't look like she was going to be able to break free.

Then, from somewhere, Julie Barlow leaped onto the bandstand, grabbed the microphone stand, and swung it at the back of Earl's head.

The stand's circular base landed on Earl's head with a solid thump. The impact was enough to make him cry out in surprise and pain and stumble forward. That loosened his hold on Felicity enough for her to break free of his grasp and run away from him, screaming.

Larry Don stood up and fired the gun in his hand. Earl went backward this time as the bullet struck him.

From the corner of his eye, Joseph saw three young men charge into the dance hall, the guns in their hands spouting flame as they sent a storm of lead clawing through the air around Larry Don. Joseph had an open firing lane and they hadn't seen him, so he dropped to one knee and started shooting, aiming low so that his rounds chopped the legs out from under the charging Wolvertons and sent them tumbling to the floor.

One of the young men managed to hang on to his gun when he fell. He was raising it to try for a shot at Joseph when Callie loomed up behind him and kicked the weapon out of his hand. She pointed the Smith & Wesson down at the three fallen men and yelled, "Don't move!"

"Same goes for you, young lady," a new voice drawled into the sudden silence that followed the gunfire.

Joseph looked around and saw a man he'd never seen before, a clean-shaven, gaunt-faced old-timer in a wheelchair being pushed by a figure Joseph *did* recognize.

"Granddaddy!" Julie exclaimed from the bandstand.

One of the Wolvertons on the floor at Callie feet said in a voice drawn tight by pain from a bullet wound, "Gramps!"

Hunched forward in the wheelchair like a buzzard, old Edgar Wolverton brandished the shotgun he held and said, "Everybody settle down! This here little dance is over!"

And so it was. Everybody who had come to Froggy's tonight to dance, drink, and flirt was gone, clearing out in a hurry once the shooting stopped. The sheriff's men might be showing up soon, drawn by reports of gunfire at the dance hall, but Callie had a hunch Sheriff Whitfield wouldn't get in too much of a rush. The sheriff would want to give things time to play out . . . and then he would tend to cleaning up the aftermath.

For now, it was just the Barlows and the Wolvertons, plus Callie, Joseph, and Froggy, who stood in between the two groups like some sort of peacemaker, although it was too late for that. The heavyset, white-haired proprietor looked distinctly nervous, too.

He got even more fidgety as he asked, "How's Earl?"

"Gone," Edgar said as he sat there in his wheelchair with the shotgun across his lap. "Larry Don drilled him clean."

"I'm sorry, but he gave me no choice, Edgar," Larry Don said. He stood with Julie and his two sons, who hadn't been injured when they were taken prisoner, flanking him. His right hand was clamped to his left shoulder, where blood showed on his shirt. "He went after my boys, and then he tried to kill me after I gave him back that little doodad he was after."

Edgar sighed. "The boy was always like that. He'd rather get what he wanted by lyin' and trickin' and hurtin' folks, instead of playin' the game straight. He never should've done the things he did, and dragged his brother and some o' his cousins into the mud with him." The old man tightened his jaw. Grief haunted his eyes as he went on, "Still, it hurts mighty bad to lose one of your own flesh and blood, even when he brought it on himself."

Edgar's chin lifted as he went on, "I'll hold no grudge against you, though, Larry Don. He was tryin' to kill you. Like you said, he left you no choice." Edgar turned to look up at the younger one standing beside and just behind him. "I'm thankful Lucas here saw the light in time to come to me and tell me what's been goin' on. He knew I wouldn't go along with some o' the dirty dealin's Earl's been up to. You know that, too, Larry Don, and you, Seth."

"Sure I do," Seth Barlow said. "That's why I agreed to come

with you and try to put a stop to things before they got too outta hand." He paused. "I'm sorry we weren't able to put a stop to it before . . . well . . ."

Edgar glanced at Earl's body, which was covered with a blanket someone had found somewhere. The three wounded young Wolvertons sat on the floor nearby, none of them with what appeared to be life-threatening injuries.

"Somehow you always know when a child's gonna come to a bad end," the old-timer said in a hollow voice. "You try and try to put 'em on the right path, but they just won't go. In the end, maybe it ain't anybody's fault 'cept for the stubborn ones who just won't listen."

Those words sounded a little sanctimonious to Callie, since she knew that the "right path" Edgar Wolverton was talking about still involved all sorts of crime. But she supposed that according to the old man's way of thinking, he had tried to do the right thing by his son and Earl was the only real villain here.

"So," Seth Barlow said, "what are we gonna do now?"

"Go back to the way things were, I suppose," Edgar said. "Our families don't like each other, and they never will. But whatever's between us, we'll leave the innocent folks out of it."

"And see to it that the law knows we didn't have anything to do with burnin' that church and desecratin' that graveyard?" Larry Don said.

Edgar sighed. "It'd pain me somethin' fierce to admit my own kin had anything to do with such things. How about you let us work that out, Larry Don? There are still some bunches around who are sorry enough to do things like that. We'll figure out a way to blame it on them, and your family's name will be cleared."

Larry Don and his father exchanged a glance. Seth nodded, and Larry Don said, "You got a deal on that, Edgar."

"All right, then. We'd best all get outta here and tend to our wounded. Howard Whitfield will be showin' up soon. When that boy's forced to get his jaws set on somethin', he hangs on like a bulldog."

Lucas moved to take hold of the handles on his grandfather's wheelchair. Edgar lifted a hand to stop him and went on, "One more thing . . . Froggy, you figure out what the damages were here tonight, and we'll take care of 'em."

"We'll pay our fair share," Seth added. "Never let it be said that the Barlows dodge any fair-and-square debts."

Froggy swallowed and nodded to both old men. "All right, fellas, I'll do that."

"Oh, and Seth . . ." Edgar added. "You might ought to put somebody besides Dennis Ordway in charge at the lodge. He's been feedin' us information and helpin' us out for a while now. Man's greedy. When money blinds a fella to family, he's got to go."

Seth nodded and said, "You ain't just a-woofin'."

Callie leaned over to Joseph and whispered, "Are they going to kill Ordway?"

"Do you really want to know?" he whispered back in a flat voice.

"Well . . . maybe not." She looked around. "What happened to Felicity and her crew? I kind of lost track of them."

Joseph frowned. "So did I. I imagine they're headed as far away from here as they can get, as fast as they can go."

The small crowd began dispersing. Julie came over to Callie and Joseph and said, "Daddy wants you to come back out to the house. He says y'all still have business to conduct."

Joseph shook his head. "He needs medical attention. So do those Wolverton boys."

"There are doctors in both families. They'll get patched up."

"Really?" Callie said, unable to contain her surprise.

"Sure." Julie smiled. "Shoot, you didn't think we were all bootlegging, redneck, backwoods outlaws, did you? There are Barlow doctors and lawyers and there's even a professor. Nobody goes into the, ah, family business unless they want to."

"What about you?"

"Me?" Julie smiled. "I'm going to be a veterinarian. I just love animals. I'm already far enough along in my studies at A&M to know that Daddy's not hurt bad. That bullet hole *does* need to be cleaned up and stitched closed, though. My cousin Frank can do that."

"Hackberry County is full of surprises," Joseph said. "Why don't we come out there tomorrow, after everything's had a chance to settle down?"

"I'll tell Daddy," Julie said with a nod. She started to turn away, then stopped and looked back at them. "It sure is hard to believe that you two have only been in these parts for a day and a half."

Callie certainly couldn't argue with that.

◆ ◊ ◆

"Barlows don't dodge fair-and-square debts," Larry Don said the next day, in the living room of the Barlow house outside of town. "My daddy said that last night, and it's the truth. I stand by the deal we made, Joseph."

"Even though it might mean you'll go to prison?" Joseph said.

He and Callie were sitting on the love seat again. Larry Don and Evelyn were the only other ones in the room. Julie and her two younger brothers had greeted the Kingfishers, then been ordered upstairs by their father.

"There's a good chance you saved my life when Jimmy, Sonny, and Carl opened fire on me," Larry Don said. "And you, Miss Callie, you saved my boys. There's a chance they would've come through it all right anyway, but we don't know that. You risked your own neck for them, and I'm not gonna forget that."

"Neither am I," Evelyn said.

Larry Don rested his right hand on that knee. His left arm was in a black silk sling, and bandages on his shoulder made his shirt bulky.

"I'm ready to go back to Corpus with you and surrender to the authorities," he declared. "If we leave before lunch, we can get there before the afternoon's over."

"I don't know," Callie said. "It doesn't seem right, somehow."

"It's just business," Joseph said. "But I appreciate you cooperating with us like this, Mr. Barlow. Even under the circumstances, I don't think we could take you into custody and return you to Nueces County against your will. You have too many friends and relatives around here for that."

Larry Don grinned. "Darned right I do. But we keep our word. Besides . . ." He chuckled. "Don't slam that big door on me just yet. Barlows have a way of dodgin' trouble . . ."

CHAPTER 24

Larry Don Barlow struck a plea deal with Nueces County prosecutors, pled guilty to delivery of stolen property, and was assessed a $50,000 fine and a five-year prison sentence, all of it suspended except for the six months he'd served in county jail awaiting trial. All the other charges against him were dropped.

When he said his goodbyes to Callie and Joseph, he promised that he would never get near enough to the coast again to smell the sea air.

"I prefer the scent of the pines," he told them.

The weeks and then the months had gone by lazily, with Callie postponing her return to California several times before finally admitting that she wanted to stay in Texas to see how Larry Don's legal situation played out.

With that over and done with, there was nothing holding her here anymore. Her leg was completely healed, and she hadn't had a nightmare in weeks.

"What *are* you going to do?" Joseph asked her as they sat

in his office. "I know you've had phone calls and emails from producers wanting to hire you again for stunt work."

She sighed as she looked out the window at the waves rolling in toward the T-Heads. "Yeah, somehow movie make-believe doesn't seem as appealing as it once did. I've enjoyed helping you out these past few months."

She had gone along with him to serve papers several times and had taken part in some cases that involved surveillance. Nothing anywhere nearly as exciting as their trip into the Piney Woods . . . but that was the thing about detective work, she had realized.

You never knew where it would lead.

"So are you actually considering staying here, getting licensed, and working with me?" Joseph leaned back in his chair behind the desk and regarded her over his steepled fingers.

"Do you *want* me to?" she asked bluntly.

"Only if *you* want to. But if you do . . ." He smiled. "I think it could prove interesting."

Callie rolled her eyes and said, "Well, with enthusiasm like that, Joey . . ."

"Welcome aboard, Callista," he said.

That evening, they were in the house on the island where they had grown up. Joseph was in the kitchen preparing supper when Callie called from the living room, "Joseph, get in here!"

He hurried into the room to find her sitting on the sofa with her laptop open on the coffee table in front of her. She gestured at the screen and told him, "Look at this."

He bent over to look and saw that she had a video paused. The words on the screen read *INSIDE BEAT*.

"Isn't that—"

"Yeah, it's a podcast. Watch!"

She tapped the touch pad to start the video. The logo dissolved into a close-up of Felicity Prosper's face as she said, "On this edition of *INSIDE BEAT: CRIME TIME SPECIAL*, the world's leading true crime podcast . . . Shootout in the Pines! The epic battle between two vicious crime families, deep in the woods of East Texas!"

The scene changed again, to the inside of Froggy's Dance Hall, with people running and screaming and guns going off. Felicity continued in a voice-over, "Live footage as this reporter risks her life to get the story for you . . . on *INSIDE BEAT!*"

"I guess that cameraman didn't run off after all," Joseph said. "He must have been hidden somewhere the whole time."

"But isn't this going to get us in trouble?" Callie asked. "Not to mention the Barlows and the Wolvertons?"

The picture broke up suddenly in a hash of colors. Nick Baker had dropped the camera and it had broken, or a wild bullet had struck it, maybe. At any rate, the few seconds of footage seemed to be all they had, since Felicity spent the rest of the podcast just talking, making the whole affair sound as lurid as possible.

She didn't have to try very hard to do that.

When it was over, Callie exclaimed, "She didn't even

mention us!"

"That's a good thing, isn't it?" Joseph said. "She probably suspected that we were mixed up in it somehow, but she didn't know for sure and didn't want to risk a lawsuit."

"I suppose so." Callie shook her head. "But you know what they say. There's no such thing as bad publicity."

"In Hollywood, maybe. But this is Texas."

Yes. Yes, it was, Callie thought. And as she realized that the night was quiet enough she could hear the surf nearby, she was very glad it was.

ABOUT THE AUTHORS

James Reasoner and Livia J. Washburn

James Reasoner has been a professional writer for over forty years. In that time, he has authored several hundred novels and short stories in numerous genres. Writing under his name, James Reasoner, and various pseudonyms, his novels have garnered praise from Publishers Weekly, Booklist, and the Los Angeles Times, as well as appearing on the New York Times, USA Today, and Publishers Weekly bestseller lists. He lives in a small town in Texas with his wife, award-winning fellow author Livia J. Washburn.

Livia J. Washburn's first story was published in 1978 in *Mike Shayne Mystery Magazine*. She received the Private Eye Writers of America Shamus Award and the American Mystery Award for her first mystery, WILD NIGHT, and a Peacemaker Award for short Western fiction, along with two nominations from Western Fictioneers. She also had a novel nominated for a Spur Award by the Western Writers of America written with her husband, James Reasoner. They live in a small town in Texas with their mutts and are very proud of their two grown daughters, who are teachers in their hometown.

James' website is http://jamesreasoner.com, and he blogs at http://jamesreasoner.blogspot.com.

Livia's website is at www.liviajwashburn.com.

Coming Soon

Kingfisher P.I. Book 2
Dark Ride

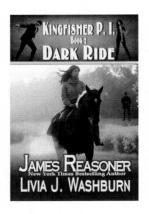

Hired to find out who's been threatening a Texas state senator's granddaughter, the two triplet sleuths Callista and Joseph Kingfisher find themselves in more trouble than they bargained for as Callie goes undercover at a therapeutic riding center and becomes involved in a dangerous conspiracy with roots on the other side of the world.

Manufactured by Amazon.ca
Acheson, AB

11946852R00127